Confessions of An IT Employee

Praise For The Book

"An amazing rom-com filled with emotions and laughter, enjoyed every bit of it. I couldn't take my eyes off the book. Every employee can relate to it."

- Economic Times

"When you write with sincerity, it sparkles like a rare gem. That's Shalini P Sawkar's book for you—an honest, frequently humorous and relatable collection of reflections that resonate with the youth.

Articulation at its best. The book's storytelling is riveting and sufficiently observational without being overbearing. The plot is sprinkled with aspirations and inspiration that keep you hooked.

Thoughtfully penned characters and a lucidly composed plot, the book is a reflection of dilemmas, desires and destiny."

- The Sunday Standard Magazine,
The New Indian Express

Confessions of An IT Employee

Shalini P Sawkar

With love,
Shalini
:)

Confessions of an IT Employee
Shalini P Sawkar

ISBN- 978-93-87780-31-6
Second Edition - 2023

Cover designed and typeset by Shalini P Sawkar
Print and bound in India by
Manipal Technologies Limited

For ajja, Srinivas B. Sawkar,
who always believed in me.

'A person often meets his destiny on the road he took to avoid it.'

- Jean de La Fontaine, Fables

One

In becoming an adult, I had meticulously lined my footsteps with those of everyone around me and steered as far away from my dream as I possibly could. But, was my dream ready to let go of me?

It was the day that sealed my fate. Oblivious to it, I woke up in my customary manner, which consisted of my mother screaming at the top of her voice from the bottom of the staircase that led to my bedroom.

"Sanchi… Sanchita!" came her voice, loud and clear.

I was twenty-two years old, and to say that by this point of time in my life my parents had grown utterly disappointed in me would be an understatement. However, I sought comfort in the knowledge that everyone my age faced the same situation.

"Yes Mama, I'm up," I yelled back. My throat was groggy and sore from the air conditioning. I rubbed the sand from my eyes and looked for my cellphone on the bed. It was 7 A.M.—a decent time for anybody to wake up. But, not for me. My college was an hour and a half away. Ergo, I was running late. I rushed through my morning activities and was downstairs in twenty minutes.

I grabbed my lunch box and bag on my way out. My parents, however, did not forget to point out in a calm yet crestfallen tone, that I was sure to miss my bus.

I was in my final year of Engineering. It was the placement season at college. Global Software Services Ltd., a well-known multinational company was coming to our college for mass recruitment. And if I missed the bus, I would fail the chance to make a first impression even before the interview.

I ran on the streets with uncombed hair and a half-open backpack. As I hurried to the bus stop, I saw a small, yellow bus leave. I shouted and ran after it. Luckily, the driver saw me and stopped by the end of the road. I crossed quickly as the roads were fairly empty in the morning, and stumbled into the bus, panting. I walked to the back and slumped my bag on my seat. It was a long ride. I sat on the bus, occasionally hopping from side to side, up and down, and hitting my head to the ceiling as the bus sped from Jayanagar to Town Hall and headed towards the north of Bangalore. I closed my eyes, and slowly drifted off.

When we were near college—I woke up to a thud as I hit my head to the ceiling. This was not uncommon—the driver had skipped a hump again. I rubbed my head until the pain subsided. Then, I started to arrange my file for the interview. I kept my resume in the first leaf and the previous semesters' mark sheets behind it. When it was five minutes to nine, a fight broke out between an auto driver and a car owner in the middle of the street. The traffic built up so quickly that we would have had to wait a good half hour to move an inch. It irked me, and everyone on the bus. We decided to take our bags and hurry on foot to college. I coughed as I walked through the sea of slow-moving vehicles and smoke. This was one of the reasons I had to make it into the company that day. Three hours of traveling every day for four years is reason enough to want to join the company close to home.

At 9:10 A.M, R. R. Institute of Technology was bustling with thousands of people coming in and out of the gates. I walked around the golden statue of the founder at the entrance, and went inside the main building, smoothing my unkempt hair. I removed my pullover and stuffed it into my bag as I waited for the lift. There were four lifts in each corner of the corridor but none of them opened for me that morning. Cursing, I walked up three floors, and finally caught a lift to the eighth.

As soon as I got off the lift, I saw a huge board—similar to a billboard—bearing the message: 'Bonanza Offer! Diamond Company! Hearty Welcome To Global Software Services Ltd.' in red, followed by a ridiculous number of exclamatory marks. I chuckled. It resembled those cheap banners at supermarkets that screamed SALE to attract customers. I, then, rushed to the other end of the corridor where the auditorium was.

In the past three years of college, I had made many friends and had lost them just as quickly. One had stayed, Nishant. I checked my phone before I opened the double doors of the auditorium—there was no message from him.

I felt a hand on my shoulder. Instantly, I turned around. It was not Nishant. It was one of my friends-turned-foe.

"You're writing the test for this company too?" she asked.

"Yes," I said, impatiently.

"But you already have an offer from another company!"

I simply looked at her, questioningly. What was she getting at? As far as I remember she had a handful of job offers herself.

"Look, my friend has not got any offers, if you could not attend this one—"

I cut her short.

"Are you telling me I have better chances of getting this job than your friend?"

She scowled but did not answer me.

"Am I snatching your friend's paper and not letting her attempt the test?" I went on, "Back off! You're no one to tell me what to do."

I stormed into the auditorium with a distracted mood. Placement season was a highly competitive time and it was not uncommon for people to try to stop others from getting the job. I shook my head to clear it.

The auditorium was filled. I looked at the heads of people in search of Nishant, and not finding him, I settled down into a seat at the back. Our auditorium was exactly like a theatre and companies were treated like celebrities. The lights were dimmed to play the video trailer of the company.

I took out my cellphone to leave him a message when Nishant came in and sat next to me.

"Nishaaa!" I called teasingly. "Where were you? I thought you weren't going to come—"

"I had some work," he said and set his bag down. The easiest way to get on my best friend's nerves was to call him by his nickname Nisha. But today, he didn't seem to care. I found it strange and wondered what was on his mind. But, the video began to play and I didn't get a chance to talk to him.

Global Software Services Ltd., founded in 1985 was headquartered in California, United States and had branches all over the world. It had fifteen offices in India out of which five were situated in Bangalore. Continuously expanding, forever providing new solutions and services to its clients, the company reported revenue of 30 billion U.S. dollars in the previous year.

"And yet they're offering us peanuts for salary," I rolled my eyes and complained to Nishant.

He nodded absently, without chuckling or whining like he usually did.

"What's the matter with you?" I asked him unable to contain myself.

"Nothing." He dismissed me.

The video showed that the company had about 2 lakh employees and more than 75,000 were in India.

Nishant came forward and whispered to me.

"I didn't pass."

I looked at him in confusion, as we hadn't had any exams then.

"Supplementary," he explained, "I got my supplementary results. I didn't clear DBMS."

I wanted to say something comforting but nothing came to my mind. I had never failed a single exam in my entire life.

"Are you allowed to attend the interview for this company?" I asked before I could stop myself. I felt like a prick. I didn't mean to belittle him; I was anxious. "What if someone comes to know?"

"No," he replied. "If anyone comes to know I won't be allowed to attend the interview for any company from now."

"But you are going to attend this?"

"Yes." He whispered. "I have to."

On the screen, the message from the CEO of the company was being played. It was followed by the clippings of happy-faced employees who shared their experiences working with the organization.

I managed to give him a small smile. "I hope you get in."

"Thanks," he said, smiling for the first time that morning.

The video also showed a sneak-peek into the infrastructure and facilities available in the multinational company—a cafeteria, a department store, library, gym, and a recreational room where one could play carom, chess or foosball! But, our delight was broken in a second when the video ended with the last slide that showed the bare-minimum CTC they were offering. This was no peanut. This was the empty shell of the peanut.

There were angry murmurs in the crowd. So the HR went on stage and explained—

"It is our company policy to disclose only basic CTC. Of course, once you join there will be the joining bonus, the six months' bonus, and various other components that will add up. Also, there's an excellent chance of a hike.

Now, shall we proceed with our process? You will be taken in two groups to the computer labs to do your aptitude test—Maths, English and Reasoning sections, 60 points, 20 questions each, and 60 minutes to complete. Any questions? No? Follow me."

I hated the aptitude tests. Why the basic math section? How would that help in deciding if a candidate deserved to join an IT company? Why wouldn't they ask computer science and coding questions?

"Why are you worried? You'll get through anyway—you are good at English and Reasoning," Nishant remarked gauging from my expression. In four years, Nishant had developed the supernatural ability to read my mind just by looking at my face—while it worked perfectly well for gossiping about a common enemy in a group or planning to bunk a class—at times like these, I wished he didn't.

He sat close by and nudged me to show him answers in the test. I told him he could see and copy whatever he wanted, but not disturb me while I was trying to answer. He copied a couple of my reasoning section answers. When it came to math, Nishant turned to his neighbor on the other side. When the timer turned red at five minutes to sixty, I submitted my answers for the aptitude test and logged out. I waited patiently for Nishant outside the computer lab. He came out looking rather pleased with himself. I supposed he had managed to flick a few more answers in the last five minutes.

"All good?"

He nodded. "I'll get through."

"Great! Come then, let's go to the canteen," I said, pulling his bag, "I'm famished."

He resisted.

"You go ahead, I'll join you," he said, "I have some work."

In the past, Nishant always asked me to accompany him everywhere. I wondered what work it was this time that he wanted to go alone. And also, he looked so serious about it.

"What work?" I asked scowling at him.

I shouldn't have asked him because his answer made me want to bite my tongue.

"I have to fill the forms for another supplementary and pay the fees," he said.

Oh right, supplementary!

I was lost for words. "Okay… so how does this work?"

"See," he said, clearing his throat "I go to the office—over there—a bald man is sitting behind the desk. I go up to him and ask sir, please give me a supplementary form—he looks me up and down and says—you failed, again? I say—siirrr. He bends down, looks in his drawer and retrieves the form."

"Really?" I asked, chuckling. "It's that simple?"

"It is," he said, shrugging his shoulders.

We burst out laughing. I shook my head. "Shut up! You know what I meant. How does the second supplementary exam work?"

"I'll have classes on the weekends. And about two to three months to prepare for the exam—I'll clear it. But, a backlog might get registered on my marks sheet,"

"Would it affect your placement?"

"I don't know. Right now, I'm using the provisional marks sheet. Just have to make sure nobody knows—"

I nodded, though I hadn't understood half the procedure he had mentioned. And I had no idea how he would manage being sneaky about a backlog.

"Shall I go with you?" I asked, pointing to the exam office.

"I'll manage."

"See you later," I waved to him and left for the canteen.

I bought myself a cup of noodles and Nishant joined me. A few minutes later, Nishant received a message from a friend that the results were put up on the placement department notice board, and we ran up with our noodles. I finished mine on the way and threw it in the bin when we reached the eighth floor.

There was a crowd around the notice board. Nishant being taller than I was could easily push through the crowd and read the names on the list, while I tried.

Both Nishant and I found our names on the list and rejoiced. There were about two hundred people selected for the interview round, I was a hundred something while Nishant was fifty-five. We still had time for our turn, and so we sat down on the staircase beside the auditorium to study. I took out a bunch of textbooks from my bag. He picked the Operating Systems one from them, and I flipped through the pages of Data Structures and C++.

A couple of hours passed, every inch of the corridor was occupied by students. The tension was palpable. Nobody ate, nobody slept and nobody went to pee unless it was absolutely necessary! Everyone was by-hearting some complicated definitions from their textbook. Now and then a volunteer called names, one by one, and minutes later, the same volunteer told them if they were selected for the HR round or not. The HR round was a given. We knew nobody would be taken out of the HR round unless they were complete psychos. So the pressure was on the technical round. After a while, I became thoroughly sick of it. I didn't want to study engineering in the first place, and I was being forced to by heart something that made absolutely no sense to me. I closed the textbook and put it in. It was six o'clock in the evening when the volunteer finally called out Nishant's name. I wished Nishant luck as he went in.

I made peace with myself that it would be the last time I would be memorizing engineering definitions. The end was near, and I had managed quite well so far. I opened my Database Management textbook again to look at some formulae when I heard someone yelling. The crowd had lessened, and I spotted a couple at one end of the corridor. They were fighting animatedly. I stared at them irritated, only to realize I knew them. I tore my eyes away from them but not before they saw me.

Shit.

Embarrassed, I tried to hide in the textbook. The girl was still looking at me, and then she got up.

"You're Sanchita, right? Dee's—I mean Deepak's friend?" she asked, looking at me.

"Yes."

"I'm Dee's girlfriend—Alisha," she said, smiling brightly at me. "We've met before."

"Yes—I remember," I lied.

I was glad she told me her name because I have a poor memory for certain-things-not-engineering. Also, I hated asking people their names when they knew mine. Again, I forgot her name almost the moment she said it and had to ask her a couple of times more that evening. She didn't mind repeating. That was the beginning of our friendship.

Alisha was gorgeous. She had caramel hair that fell in cascades to her shoulders. They matched the colour of her eyes. And, I wondered why she would be interested in a guy like Deepak. But, I knew better than to ask her that in our first meeting.

Nishant came out of the interview room.

"How was it?" I asked eagerly. He didn't say anything; his forehead was creased with lines of worry and he constantly looked at the door. The volunteer came out holding a register.

"Nishant," he said.

Nishant stood up, crossing his fingers.

"You may leave, now. You're done for the day," he said in a bored, diplomatic tone.

Shit.

Nishant stood rooted to the spot. Everybody was looking at him. He cursed under his breath. He looked at me, embarrassedly. I wished I could say something comforting to him, but I didn't.

He drew in a sharp breath and bent down to pick his bag up. I was still trying to find words to console him, but he saved me that trouble. He didn't look at me.

"Bye," he said to me as he left.

He was doomed. Now, the backlog would no longer be hidden on his profile and he wouldn't be allowed to attend any more campus interviews. No company wanted a candidate with a backlog. That was the basic criterion. I felt a pinch in my stomach.

I was distracted from my thoughts when the volunteer called out my name. I shook my head to clear it and said a quick prayer. I stumbled on the staircase and went inside the auditorium catching my heavy black file.

My interviewer looked bored. He motioned for me to come in and take the seat. The chair made a noise as I clumsily pulled it and sat. I then smacked the file on the desk, unintentionally, and straightened myself, hoping he hadn't noticed.

"Been waiting for a long time, ha?" he asked.

"Yes… No—" I didn't know what to answer. He nodded and asked to see my file. I lifted it as carefully as I could, unlocked it, and handed the open file to him.

He asked me to tell him about myself. I did.

He told me to speak loudly and asked me if I had eaten anything.

"Yes, I have," I answered, embarrassedly.

But, he went on to ask me if I would like to eat some cake. Only then I noticed the small piece of cake and a cup of coffee on the table. I declined, politely.

The rest of the interview went on smoothly. He asked me a couple of Operating system questions, which I answered correctly. I fidgeted around a few programming codes, but I guess he overlooked them because I was selected for the next round.

As I left the room, he warned me that I would have to be loud if I wanted to survive in IT. I agreed in my loudest voice possible, thanked him and left. I didn't think much of his advice then. It was the one I needed the most. But, at that moment I was relieved I had cleared the interview.

Two

It was the last day of college. I was quite glad the four-year journey was coming to an end. However, there was one person I was going to miss terribly, and so I planned to celebrate with him after the exam.

Of course, we would still meet after college ends, but since we both lived on opposite ends of the city, not as often.

Nishant had cleared his backlog and was even placed in a multinational company in the campus placements. Astonishingly, the placement department had neither discovered his backlog, nor the lies in his resume. But that was one of Nishant's infamous talents—to slip through your fingers unnoticed. He managed to keep the news of his 'F' grade hidden at home as well—by checking the mailbox every morning for his performance record—even with two sisters and three brothers, all older than him, keeping a close watch on him. Therefore, what he was about to do did not surprise me.

After our exam, we went to get our provisional marks sheet attested and signed by the Head Of Department. Nishant had not received his changed performance record for the previous semester yet. Therefore, his performance record still showed the backlog. He had planned to slip his provisional marks sheet discreetly among the others' marks sheets on the

HOD's table, and leave it there for his signature. But, this plan was soon canceled as the HOD was in his cabin when we entered.

My heart was beating fast. I had no idea how Nishant was going to get away with it now. He moved closer to me and caught me by the arm before I entered.

"Be cool," he whispered. "Don't act like you are doing something wrong."

I nodded.

"Sir," I said, opening the translucent door but an inch. "May I come in?"

The HOD lifted his head from the register he was filling and nodded. Nishant entered after me.

"Sir, we wanted our provisional marks sheets to be signed for the background verification," I said and handed him my provisional marks sheet.

"Original?" he asked, extending his other hand.

I gave him the original marks sheets of the past semesters. I glanced at Nishant; he was pretending to be adjusting his previous marks sheets in order. I tried not to look at him again, as I didn't want to raise suspicion. The HOD checked each of my marks sheets and tallied it with the grades that I had filled in the consolidated provisional marks sheet. Once he was completely satisfied with his inspection, he signed my provisional marks sheet.

"So, you cleared the training test then?"

For sake of efficiency and reduction of cost to the company, the multinational company Global Software Services Ltd. had decided to give the foundation training for joining the corporate world in our college campus itself, during the last term. It had taken me three attempts to pass the test at the end of the training, despite my thorough mugging up of the subjects. After the second failed attempt, I had tallied my answers with a girl who had passed and we had discovered that most of my answers were right. Something strange was going on—so I had decided to casually mention it to my HOD and find out his opinion. But when I had reached his cabin, I had discovered that I was not alone. One boy was clearly stating that he had copied every single answer from another, and the other boy had passed while he had failed. The HOD had rolled his eyes at him, and then he had come up with a theory that the software application was faulty in the sense that it was not accepting the answers near the closing time. So, he had advised us to submit our answers early in the next attempt. One would think that a software company would at least be able to develop its software application correctly and run it without any errors, especially a critical online test application, that would affect millions of new joiners. But…

"Yes sir," I said. "I submitted it twenty minutes early this time and I passed."

"I told you!" he said, with a grin.

Whether his theory was true or not, he certainly took pride in it. And, as for me, since it had worked in my case, I didn't have any reason not to believe him.

"Next?" he asked, with an outstretched arm.

Nishant handed him his provisional marks sheet and the originals of past semesters. He was doing a good job of keeping a straight face as the HOD tallied his first and second-semester grades with the provisional one. My heart was beating faster, and I wondered if I should go outside and wait, but Nishant gave me a stern look and I refrained from any sort of movement.

At that moment, the door clicked open and the HOD's assistant peeped inside.

"Sir, you're still here?" said the assistant. "It's two-thirty."

The HOD looked at him in confusion.

"I beg your pardon sir, I had gone for lunch and I forgot to remind you earlier," the assistant went on. "You have the Department Heads' Meeting at two-thirty."

"Right," said the HOD, as he handed Nishant back his provisional marks sheet. "Telephone them. I'll be there immediately."

"Sir, please," said Nishant, thrusting his provisional marks sheet back at the HOD. "It won't take a minute."

"You can leave it on my table Nishant, I'll check and sign it later," said the HOD standing up to leave.

"Sir, you can check it now," he said, thrusting the bundle of original marks sheets at the HOD. "Today is the last day of document submissions for Prime Technologies. They're going to start the background verifications from tomorrow. Please?"

"Quick," the HOD agreed.

Nishant showed him each semester marks sheets one by one, pointing at the final grades in each and the provisional. When it came to the last, he showed a different semester marks sheet once again. The HOD, in his hurry to leave, did not notice this and signed his provisional marks sheet without any hesitance.

I couldn't believe Nishant's luck. I bit my lip from smiling at him. He was still maintaining a poker face!

"Get it attested from my assistant—the college seal," said the HOD, pointing at his assistant as he left.

"Thank you, sir."

Nishant and I did not dare look at each other or express glee since we still needed to keep the act going—for the sake of the cocky assistant. The assistant made a few inquiries himself before attesting our provisional marks sheets with the college seal, but we managed without letting him know of Nishant's secret.

"You're one lucky ass!" I told him the moment we were out of earshot.

"It's called talent," he scoffed, with a lop-sided grin.

"Talent!" I laughed, and called out to the fast disappearing silhouette of the HOD, "Sir! He's cheating—"

"Hush," he said, closing my mouth and walked me in the other direction.

We went out of the building through the back entrance, down the familiar stairs and reached the grounds. It was a hot, fine day. I was still laughing when he said—

"You look stunning today. Blue suits you."

He complimented me so rarely that when he did, I knew it was genuine, and I gracefully accepted it. I had taken care to wake up early that morning. I wore my favourite blue top, black jeans and brushed my generally-messy-hair till it glistened: a single pin held it on top and my hair fell in curls to my waist.

"Thank you," I said, slowly glancing at him. I sometimes got this feeling that he liked me. Did I like him? I didn't know. He was undoubtedly attractive. He was tall, lean and had piercing eyes. But, did I like him? I still didn't know.

We walked the length of the college grounds when Nishant let out a sigh and asked.

"So, how is Raghav?"

I was taken aback. I had met Raghav during a college festival a few months ago. We bonded over some event, but our friendship ended as quickly as it had begun when Raghav asked me if I wanted to be his girlfriend and I had refused. The last I had heard of him was that he was interning at a software company in Chennai.

"How would I know?" I said, shrugging my shoulders, more indignantly that I wanted to. "I'm not in touch with him."

I stole a glance at Nishant and wondered if he knew that Raghav had asked me out.

"As if!" he scoffed, "What do you think of him?"

He knew. I groaned inwardly. He would never stop teasing me.

"I don't think of him," I said. "Where are we going today? Pizza?"

"We're going to Coffee Day," said Nishant, pulling me toward the street outside the gate of the college. Our campus was huge and it took us about twenty minutes to get to the gate.

"Coffee day? But I'm hungry—we didn't have lunch—"

We had stopped going to Coffee Day since the first year. Nishant often chided that it was coffee in a fancy outfit with an unpronounceable Italian or French name for it. I wondered where the sudden love for Coffee Day had come from.

"You can eat samosa or sandwich," he said, casually. I was not buying it. When I probed further, he merely shrugged it off saying, "Just like that."

Still, my curiosity didn't die. Was he taking me on a date? I wondered. I admonished myself the moment that thought crossed my mind. What was wrong with me? Ugh. Perhaps, it was nothing, and he merely wanted a cold coffee. It was a hot day. A zillion other possibilities plagued my mind while we crossed the street and reached the café on the other side. His stride became faster as we reached the door, so much so that he almost raced me to it. I laughed, as I reached the door. I liked being childish about him. My laughter wiped away as I realized he was not racing me to it, but he was holding it open for me. It was quite strange. I pretended not to notice and walked through. Normally he would push the door in my face and barge inside, and if I protested, he would mock me for being slow. Chivalry was an alien concept to him, and so I found his behavior peculiar when he pulled out the armchair for me inside the café and offered to go to the counter to place our orders.

"Why are you being so generous?"

On other days, he would slump in a chair and behave like he was doing me a favour by catching me a seat opposite him on the table while I went to place our order.

"It's the last day," he said, grinning sheepishly. "Thought I should be nice to you."

"Not going to say no to that!" I said and sat back in the purple armchair. "I'll have a Devil's Own, and a vegetable sandwich."

The café was now bustling with patrons and smelled of cold air, coffee, and cake. But, I had a cozy table at the far end from where I watched people walk by through the tinted glass of the café. A thought that had been popping up in my head from quite some time, and no matter how much I tried to subdue it, it kept coming back. So, when Nishant came back, I jumped straight to the point.

"You haven't told me about your love life in a long time," I said.

Nishant shot me a look but didn't say anything.

The waitress arrived with a glass of coffee lacquered with chocolate sauce and whipped cream, and a dollop of vanilla ice cream on top. The whimsical sight of my coffee instantly lifted my spirit. I waited, while she laid the cappuccino in front of him, and a plate of sandwiches between us and left.

"Do you like someone?" I ventured again, sipping my drink. He let out a small chuckle and shook his head. "Who's your new crush? C'mon, tell me."

When he didn't answer for the second time, I began to worry. If he were in love with me, it would change everything between us. He was my best friend—he was the one I went to when I had a crush on someone else or fought with my ex—he was like my wingman and my agony aunt—all that would change, and we would end up fighting like couples. I didn't want that. I had to think of a way to slip out of this without hurting his feelings.

"What about you?" he asked, pulling me out of my reverie. "Who's your latest crush?"

"Nobody," I said quickly. I regretted saying it a second later. I should've told a name, what if he proposed to me? I was so jittery to find a way to change the conversation that I ended up blurting out—"Why did you ask me about Raghav, earlier?"

There was nothing else that came to my mind. I knew I had to stall him from proposing to me. It was a matter of weeks—he would forget about it, have a crush on someone else, and move on.

Nishant gave me a look and slowly chewed on his sandwich. I didn't know what to make of it, he was still staring at me, and a slow smile touched his lips as if he knew I was deliberately changing the subject. I licked my lips that were dry and looked hither thither. He set down his sandwich, cleared his throat and said in a low tone, "Because he called me."

"WHAT?" Why would Raghav call Nishant? They hardly know each other!

"He wanted to know about you," said Nishant, emptying a packet of sugar in his cappuccino.

"Know about me?" I couldn't for the life of me figure out why the fella couldn't ask me if he wanted to know about me? I ground my teeth and tried to keep my cool.

"He asked about the kind of movies you like, music, presents, and so on," said Nishant. "I think he wants to surprise you."

"I'm surprised already, thank you very much," I said, my hand went to my head and I smoothed my hair. I despised surprises! "Listen, I don't know if you know this, but he asked me out. And, I refused… I don't understand… How did he even find your number?"

"He asked you out?" chuckled Nishant. "I'm not surprised. I told you—from the beginning he was hitting on you."

"I didn't believe it," I sighed, sipping my coffee.

"He found me on Facebook," said Nishant, finishing the last of his sandwich. "He pinged me there and asked for my number."

"Listen," I said. "Don't encourage him with any of it."

He nodded. "You know, when he asked me all that yesterday—that's when I realized how well I know you."

He said it so earnestly that I didn't believe there was any intention or agenda behind it, and so, I gave him a warm smile and nodded. I had finished my sandwich by then, and we left the café. We walked the length of Old B.E.L. road, in the soft drizzles of May, remembering our four-year journey, and being happy for we never had to study again. I did not know my happiness was short-lived.

When we turned the corner, he waved good-bye to me. He was lanky, drenched and stood to shake the droplets of water off his hair. The sun had not set yet, and if I saw correctly, I thought I caught a hint of a rainbow in the sky behind him. I gave him a warm smile. I waved good-bye and left. That was it, a farewell to four years of friendship.

I went home to find my inbox filled with unread emails. Hidden amidst the advertisements, an email caught my eye—call letter for Global Software Services.

Three

The joining date was two weeks away. That meant I wouldn't have a summer vacation after my final year, but I didn't complain. I would start earning! I couldn't be more thrilled. I'll be honest, four years ago, my reason for joining engineering was based on the biggest myth: that engineers earned a mint! Now, I know the reality of it: that engineers earned enough to buy a piece of mint. Even then, I was enthusiastic about getting my first bank account. Within a week I opened my bank account, though I had zero knowledge of it previously, filed for my PAN card, got my Aadhar card and various other documents ready. My parents had never seen me taking responsibility earlier and I think they were relieved.

My office would begin the next day. It was midnight; I sat on my bed, sleepless evaded me. Nishant had not spoken to me since the last day. I was so afraid of messing up our friendship, that I had done just that. I picked up the phone and dialed him. It was not uncommon for me to dial him at this hour. We had often called each other at night during exams to stay awake and study. Please be awake, I whispered into my phone. On the fifth or sixth ring, he picked up.

"Hello," he said in a groggy voice.

"Hi," I said, smiling into my speaker. "How are you?"

"I was happily dozing on my bed until you—you called to ask how I am at this hour?"

"Shut up," I said, chuckling. I felt no guilt in waking him up. "Listen, I got my call letter. It's my first day tomorrow."

"Call letter? I got it too. What's the big deal?" he spoke fast, "So when's the joining date?"

I rolled my eyes. "Are you not listening to me? I said it's tomorrow!"

"Oh," he said, suddenly awake. "Big news. Good luck. Buh-bye..."

"I'm the one who needs to be up by seven tomorrow. What are you whining about?"

He asked me if I knew any of the people joining with me the next day, I said no. It was one of the things I was tensed about. He reassured me that it would be fine, and I would make some good friends.

"You think so?"

"Yes, so where do you report tomorrow, the Bellandur branch or the one in Jayanagar?" he asked.

"Neither," I said, "The orientation programme is in Taj Vivanta."

I heard him gasp.

"Stupid Prime Technologies!" he cursed, "We have nothing like that for our first day."

It was half-past twelve by the time I got off the phone with Nishant. It felt like old times. And, I peacefully went to bed after that.

The next morning I was ready by eight. Dressed in a pair of grey cotton pants and a pink striped top, I wore a pair of uncomfortable formal shoes and hoped I didn't have to wear them for the rest of the year. I carried a black file with me in which I had placed all my documents. I got in the car and asked the driver to drive to Taj Vivanta on M. G. Road. I lived on the south side of Bangalore and it took me about twenty-thirty minutes to reach the hotel. This was heavenly compared to the two-hour journey to college, and I was glad to be rid of that college bus. I could finally start using the family car to go to the office.

I reached the venue early. I walked inside, careful not to slip on the marble floor in my new shoes. The staff looked at the file in my hand and directed me to an auditorium on the first floor. My first instinct was to look for Alisha as the people started filling in. But then, the chances of meeting her were thin. She might have received a different joining date, or a different joining location even if it was today. That was when I met Bhoomija. She was completely different from me, dressed in salwar kameez and tying her hair in a single braid. She was slightly plump. I was quick to judge her as a village mutt. Who wears jhoomka earrings and glass bangles for an office event? But little did I know that she was judging me too, as a spoilt, dimwit brat from the city.

"Where are you from?" I asked her after a while to initiate a conversation. The On-Boarding was a long process and we were to stay there the whole day, signing numerous documents and listening to drab speeches, so I figured I might as well speak to the girl sitting next to me.

"I'm from Palamaner," she said.

"Oh," I said, wondering where on earth Palamaner was. Karnataka? Tamil Nadu? Kerala, perhaps. "Where is that?"

"You don't know Palamaner?" she asked, a tad condescendingly. "Have you heard of Chittoor?"

"No," I replied.

"Have you heard of Andhra Pradesh?" she asked this time, loudly. "I'm from there!"

Jeez. I rolled my eyes at her. What was the need to get so worked up about it? As if she could hear my thoughts, she softened up and added—

"It's a village to the south of Andhra. Quite close to Karnataka."

I smiled, and well, our conversation went on effortlessly for the rest of the day, although when I told her I was from Bangalore, she did give me one of her condescending looks again and said—

"I thought so."

We soaked in the grandeur of the place when we were taken into the banquet hall for lunch. During the meal, I found out Bhoomija did not like reading novels for fun, did not understand Hindi movies and watched English movies on rare occasions. While I tried to find something to bond over, I thought it best to avoid asking her about television series or music—I knew what she would answer—instead, I asked her about her home. Her eyes lit up instantly, she told me she was an only child to her parents, and that they were landowners in the village. She had grown up eating fresh food from her farm and hated the stale food that her paying guesthouse now provided. I decided to pull her for a second helping of papads and pakodas. Then we ate a plateful of desserts.

Later, for a couple of days, we were taken to various luxury hotels across Bangalore and fed sumptuous food. We delighted over it unaware that we were being raised like sheep for the slaughter.

"Isn't bonded labour banned in India?" I asked her, post-lunch, examining the document in my hand.

"For forty years now," she replied.

"Yet, here we are, being made to sign a bond of fifteen months not to leave the company."

If we did leave in the first six months, we would have to pay the company up to 75,000 rupees, in other words, more than the company would pay us. And after that, the penalty would go on reducing. It made me queasy. It felt more like imprisonment and a lot less like employment.

We signed some more NDAs and tax forms. The HR warned us against watching adult content on the office computer. As if anyone would be dumb enough to do that, but to my surprise, the HR went on to say that he had fired a few people in the past because of it. Even YouTube, movie sites, torrents, Facebook and all other social media sites were banned. The HR ended his speech, and with that our fate was sealed for the next one-and-a-half year.

Though we had completed one set of training courses given by Global Services in college, we had to take another training, where we were divided randomly, with no regard to our branch of education or interest, and put into different domains. Bhoomija and I were put in the same domain—Enterprise management software. I, a computer science engineer, with a history of good scores, obviously felt entitled to coding. I wanted to create something. I didn't slog four years in B.E. to merely maintain and support a pre-existing module. A few vain attempts to get my domain changed, brought my head back where it belonged. I contented myself to submit to the domain that I was given, and focus on passing the training test. Having been acquainted with Global Software Services' testing software in my college days, I was more afraid than others that I would fail the test for no fault of mine. However, Bhoomija and I submitted our answers before anyone else and passed the test. I had tipped her about the timer, and server issues of the test software.

Bhoomija did not wear her glass bangles anymore. She had even begun to tie her hair in a ponytail instead of a braid. We sat in the cafeteria outside, getting some sun while the others struggled with their tests. I was sipping my cold coffee when she nudged me.

"You missed. He was so cute!" she squealed.

In the past week, Bhoomija had pointed out a dozen guys she felt were cute. I'm not proud of it, but for a while, this had become our favourite pass-time. When I looked up from my coffee, I saw the silhouette of a tall man disappear into the building in the direction she pointed. It looked like he had a beard, but I couldn't say for sure.

"Listen, forget that. Why don't we go to a movie?" I didn't think she would agree but I had to try. "We have the whole day to ourselves."

"What if someone found out?"

"Nobody knows us. Haven't you ever bunked classes in college?"

"Bunk? I studied Engineering in Palamaner. Do you think anyone—"

"Fine, I get it. Look, this is easier than bunking college. We don't have any work, we have clocked in this morning, and we can clock in after the movie."

"What if we get a project call?"

"We won't. But, if you're still scared, you can connect the office mail to your phone," I told her, and she was convinced. She gave me her phone. "Shall I book the tickets for Sonam Kapoor's Khoobsurat then?"

Once I connected the office mail to her phone, she agreed, on the condition that I explain the movie to her, as her Hindi was rotten. We caught an auto-rickshaw to an INOX theatre in the vicinity and settled in with a bucket of chili popcorn. Twenty minutes into the movie and Bhoomija had not asked me to translate anything. Perhaps, she wasn't as bad at Hindi as she claimed to be. But, it turned out that she was more interested in Sonam's dresses than the dialogues. She pulled my sleeve, during a song.

"Do you have such dresses?" she asked, excitedly. "Do you wear them in Bangalore?"

"Yes," I shrugged. It was a simple frock. I didn't see why she was fussing over it.

"You're so lucky," she squealed. "In my village, we must wear *lehenga, blouse,* and *dupatta.*"

"Are you serious?"

"We are not even allowed to wear *salwar kameez,*" she whispered over the sound of the movie.

"That's ridiculous!" I knew that people in the rural regions stuck to traditional Indian attire, but *salwars* were part of it. How bizarre! I offered to go to the mall with her.

During intermission, Bhoomija looked into her phone and gasped.

"Check your inbox."

She had received a project call in the office mail.

Shit!

I had received it too, an hour ago. Both of us had been locked into an alcoholic beverage project named Popshake. I reread the mail to make sure it was a project-call.

"It's alright, don't panic."

Of course, she panicked. She dropped her phone, stumbled in the seat to pick it up, and kept looking for something on it. "I told you we shouldn't have bunked." She found what she was looking for.

"What are you doing? Don't call them—" I said snatching her phone. "Look, we'll send them an email asking for the location. We don't even know if it's in Bangalore—"

"It *is* in Bangalore!"

"Oh alright," I said I had already found the location by checking the project manager's location on the mail, and it was 20kms away. "But it's in Ecospace, Bellandur! That's like two hours from here. We can't go there now. Let's ask them the exact location and inform them that we will be joining tomorrow."

"It doesn't work like that. I should never have listened to you," she snatched the phone from me and rang them. "I'll ask if we can join by tomorrow."

The movie had resumed, and I pulled her outside the screening room. Someone picked up on the other end, and Bhoomija's face went paler by the second. "We are in the Jayanagar office now," she said, and I let a sigh of relief that she didn't let slip in her fright that we had gone for a movie. "But—yes—okay. Thank you."

I looked at her inquiringly.

"We are dead," she declared. "Come, we don't have much time. We have to immediately catch the inter-company shuttle and go to Ecospace."

"But," I looked in the direction of the theatre. "The movie is still—"

"CHUCK the movie," she snapped.

We took an auto-rickshaw back to the office and caught the intercompany shuttle before it took off. I say 'took off' because the intercompany shuttle assumed itself to be an airplane that could zoom across the city at high speed, nearly knocking down anyone who came in its way, bumping and scraping its bottom on every hump on the road. I clenched my jaw when the driver the hit brakes—I dashed into the seat in front of me—only to gain speed back the next second and I was thrown back into my seat. This happened so often that it made my college bus seemed like a blissful toy train.

"The lady yelled at me over the phone saying we should've reported to Bellandur office by ten this morning," she said, looking into her watch. It was four 'o clock.

"We received the mail at 1 P.M. We didn't have a project before that," I said. "And, we were taking up that training test at ten."

I daresay I was a little disappointed when I found out that Bhoomija and I were going to be in the same project. Albeit, she was not as uptight as she used to be, she still was different from me. But, I suppose it was better than having nobody. The bus crossed a signal and I had my first glimpse of Agara Lake. Its blue-grey waters shimmered in the afternoon sun making it look like flowing silk. A thick band of vegetation surrounded the lake, offering a bit of country vibe in the middle of the city. Most of the lakes in Bangalore are dried up, so whenever I came across a good one, I cherished the moment. I tore my gaze from the white birds that were sipping the water there when the bus turned another bend and climbed a flyover. Below the flyover, on my right, was RMZ Ecospace. Finally! Bhoomija was fumbling for something in her bag.

"God! I hope they don't take another interview before taking us into the project. I haven't prepared—I hope she doesn't screw us for coming late—"

"Relax…" I said, slipping my bag on my right shoulder. My bag was extremely light. It contained a lunch box and a notebook. I got off the death-mobile, hoping never to climb it again. "We'll explain…"

We flashed our ID cards to the guard, and he let us in. RMZ Ecospace was a huge campus, with a miniature fountain at the entrance, lined with palm trees on either side of the pathway, a shrubbery here and there, and several IT companies. At four in the noon, the pathway was deserted, except for one or two catering vans. Global Software Services was at the far end of the campus, the last building. It was a giant green trapezium of tinted glass. As soon as we gave the name Popshake to the receptionist, she pointed to the elevator and said the fifth floor.

This was it: my first project. At that time, I had no idea it would also be my last. I could hear my heartbeat, there was a pulse throbbing in my throat. I took a deep breath and pulled the handle of the glass door on the fifth floor. It didn't open. I tried harder. I pushed it. The glass door shook, but it didn't open. Then, it struck me.

Bhoomija laughed at me.

"You need to swipe—"

"I know," I cut her short.

"And I thought I was nervous…"

I walked embarrassedly to the tiny grey box to the side of the door, flashed my ID, and the door unlocked. Bhoomija was still chuckling. Together we walked four steps and stopped. We had no idea where to go. There were a hundred people on this floor, sitting at their desks, and moving about here and there. I looked at Bhoomija accusingly as if this was her fault the both of us were here, and now she must correct it. Hesitantly, Bhoomija approached the person on the first desk. He shooed her off within a second. And, Bhoomija came back to my side. I nodded. We then walked past rows of desks, hoping to find a non-busy person. We hadn't come across the words "visibility" and "pretense" in IT terms, and hence we assumed each one of them staring at their computer screens was genuinely busy. Bhoomija spotted a middle-aged lady in the last row.

"Hello," said Bhoomija. "We are new here—new joiners..."

"So?" She looked up from her screen. "What do you expect me to do? What are you going to do joining this project? The ones already in here don't work efficiently—can't you see I'm busy?"

Bhoomija gulped. "Sorry, we'll come back later—"

"Fill your forms. Go somewhere... make yourself useful. Go," she barked.

Bhoomija looked around, and timidly pointed to an empty desk in the corner with no computers, "We'll be there."

"Perfect," snapped the woman, giving us a thumbs-up.

When we were out of earshot, Bhoomija said, "I'm quite sure she was the one I spoke to on the phone."

"I don't doubt it," I said.

After an hour of staring at people and machines, we saw the middle-aged woman walk toward us, with another lady scampering to keep up with her.

"Kavana, I want you to meet these new joiners. You were looking for freshers right?"

"Yes, yes," panted a petite Kavana. She came up to the middle-aged woman's shoulder even with her two-inch pump heels. She was exceedingly fair and her face was a clean slate; she had huge black eyes smeared with kohl and fat blood-red lips.

"This is your Team Lead, Kavana." Kavana gave us a broad smile and a small hand to shake. "Welcome to Popshake."

The middle-aged lady told us—"Give me your forms, have you signed them?"

Bhoomija and I exchanged looks. We hadn't asked her the forms earlier out of fear that she might yell at us.

"You haven't taken your forms? How irresponsible—"

"Shree," said Kavana to the middle-aged lady. "Let me handle it from here. I'll give them the forms and get it signed from them, don't worry—"

Clad in light blue salwar kameez, and donning matching jewelry my first impression of Kavana that evening was that she was Cinderella's fairy godmother who had come to our rescue.

*

The first month was the hardest: day-by-day Bhoomija and I began to realize how inconsequential we were to the company, how little we mattered to our project, and how unnoticeable we were to our team. Then, we got used to the idea.

At first, we were given a single computer system to share, in other words, stare at, since we had no work. During this time, the KT- Knowledge Transfer sessions took place, where a couple of seniors gave presentations that flew over our heads faster than Jet airways. In one session the lights in the conference room had been switched off to enhance the projector light. Bhoomija had dozed off. The senior-most manager had made the presentation that morning, and Kavana had given Bhoomija livid looks when the lights had been switched back on. For weeks after that, we were given menial tasks such as filling irrelevant data on Excel sheets and deleting millions of unwanted files. I wondered if it was a consequence of her dozing. Our fingers ached from pressing the delete key so much, that at one point, Bhoomija decided to keep her water bottle on the delete button of the keyboard and let it run continuously.

I was finally given a computer of my own, and that too beside Bhoomija, as the woman who previously worked on it had moved out of the project. On the other side of Bhoomija sat a middle-aged manager, Chetan, who liked to presume he was a teenager. He spiked his hair, listened to English radio on the office computer with his blue Beats by Dr. Dre headphones, and mostly acted smug. Today, he peeped into Bhoomija's screen, while the bottle still hung on the delete key, as he often did and gave us a thumbs-up.

"Great work, ha?"

We gave him a pasted smile. As if we couldn't sense his sarcasm! I decided to have some fun; I leaned in my seat so Chetan could see me past Bhoomija and the cardboard-like separator on my desk.

"So Chetan, you like Dr. Dre, ha?" I asked him. As expected, Chetan gave me a puzzled look, and said—"Doctor who?"

I laughed inwardly and bit my lip to hide my smirk.

"Great headphones, by the way," I remarked, and showed him a thumbs-up.

Even then, he didn't get it, he gave me a wide grin and said, "It's cool, isn't it?" and threw in a few hand gestures to go with it.

I could no longer hold my laughter. I had my cheap thrills. Although he could accessorize himself like a teenager, his knowledge compared to a teenage kid was zilch.

Meanwhile, the bottle was also noticed by a senior in our team on his way to the washroom. Surprisingly, he didn't stop us from doing it. I suspect Bhoomija had a crush on him, as she had made meticulous attempts to look smart in front of him on previous occasions. But, sadly she seemed puerile. She quickly removed the bottle from the key and slapped her forehead, regretfully. Tarun simply shook his head and gave us a lopsided grin.

After deleting about thirty thousand redundant files, I'd had enough of it, I called Bhoomija for a cup of tea downstairs in the canteen, but she refused.

"Come on, it's not like we are doing anything important," I urged her. "Nobody cares whether we delete those files or not! Look, even Kavana isn't there on her desk right now."

"What if Kavana comes back?"

"So what if she does? We are allowed to take coffee breaks!"

"No, you go—I'll be here," she said.

I went back to my system and hit Lync, an online office messenger, and I wondered if I knew anyone else in the Bellandur office.

Alisha!

I didn't know which branch she reported to. I typed Alisha in the search bar and a thousand results popped up. Right, I punched my desk; the problem was I didn't even know her last name. I hated Bhoomija's irrational fears of the corporate world; she took one break throughout the day, for lunch, and that too for just twenty minutes. And I was sick of sitting by myself in the canteen. I had to find someone to hang out with. Alisha… Alisha… Alisha Wellington, Alisha Erakat, I kept scrolling through. Then I checked them by their work locations, New York, Florida, Australia, Philippines, New Delhi. Could this be her? No, please don't be relocated to Delhi, I whispered to the screen and scrolled down some more. I cursed myself for not asking her phone number that day.

Alisha C. Patel, work location: Bangalore.

I pinged her.

Four

"Your friend is an eye candy!"

Chetan remarked as soon as I came back to my seat. When I met Alisha in the canteen, I had seen him stop dead in his tracks and stare at us. It had seemed peculiar then as he had carried on without saying a word, but it's perfectly clear now. He was watching me expectantly, so I nodded.

"Yes, she is." It struck me then. The seat next to mine was empty. "Where is Bhoomija?"

Chetan squinted at me in confusion and then, remembering, he turned his nose in distaste. "Your lady with that rat-like face," he said snapping his fingers hastily.

"Kavana?" I couldn't believe he called her a *rat!* I wanted to tell him what his face looked like, but his answer brought me back to my problem at hand.

"Yes," he snapped his finger louder and pointed at me in triumph. "She took her away."

Shit.

I grabbed a pen and book from my bag and went in the direction he pointed: the conference rooms. I searched the sea of meeting rooms at the other end of the floor; tentatively peeping into some, pressing my face against the frozen glass of other rooms, until I finally spotted the people I was looking for. I opened the door an inch and peered inside. Kavana's eyes fell on me instantly, but mine turned to Bhoomija. There was also another person in the room. Tarun. What was *he* doing at the meeting?

"Look who finally showed up!" said Kavana, her mouth curled up in disdain. "If you're done with your coffee and pastries et cetera, care to join us?"

I stumbled inside and pulled a chair out. The chair promptly creaked to embarrass me further. I blurted some excuse but Kavana dismissed it, and the expression in her eyes softened. Or, so I imagined.

It was freezing inside the room. I closed my arms and rubbed, silently looking for the AC vent. Not that I would dare ask them to switch it off, if only I could look at it and curse in my mind, I would be satiated.

Bhoomija leaned towards me and whispered. "I tried calling you but your phone didn't connect…"

"As we've discussed, I'll have a word with our manager," said Kavana, looking at Bhoomija. "I'll be shifting you both to the CRM team from tomorrow."

It was my turn to look at Bhoomija with my jaw dropping to the table. She was looking straight ahead, impassively. As Kavana went on about the team, I nudged Bhoomija. Kavana caught my eye.

"Yes?"

I looked to Bhoomija for support but she offered me none. I couldn't place it but something about it seemed like a sham to me. I gathered my courage and asked. "We were trained in Sales applications when we joined Global Services. I don't know anything in CRM, it would be tough to work on—"

"So, you don't want to shift your team? Isn't that what you're getting at?" Kavana cut me short. "Can't believe the kids these days—I try to do something good for them, and they question me instead," she said to Tarun, who sat beside her on the other side of the white table. I could feel my palms sweat, and Bhoomija's accusing eyes.

"Look, CRM is one of the most sought after applications in the world! It's a hot skill. You'll get paid in millions outside, once you learn it. Do you have any idea how many people are dying to be on that team—right here, in our project—but they're not lucky enough to get the opportunity!" Kavana spoke to me as if I was an eight-year-old child who had misbehaved.

"I—I was worried that I didn't get trained in CRM—how would I handle the work?" I said slowly.

"That is precisely why you have Tarun here!" Kavana squealed, patting him on the back. "He's the best resource we've had till now in CRM. He knows the inside out of the system like the back of his hand—he'll train you guys."

Bhoomija kicked me under the table. I knew what she wanted me to say. From the corner of my eye, I could see the colour rising up her cheeks.

"Kavana, stop. You're embarrassing me," Tarun gave us one of his most disarming smiles and teased, "although, I hope you'll remember that during the year-end ratings."

A grimace crossed Kavana's face and it was gone in a fraction of a second, but not before I missed it. "I've been asking you to teach me—but—anyway, I hope you do a better job with these guys."

"Don't worry, I'll teach them," he winked at us, "I do know the system inside out."

I'm not sure when I had conceded, but Kavana never asked me again. She simply tapped the table, gave us a big grin and said, "So, that's settled then. Tomorrow, sharp at10 o'clock we'll start your CRM training. You can leave."

"But Kavana, I'm on shift," I heard Tarun say as we walked out the door. "My shift doesn't begin till eleven-thirty."

"Come early for a few days."

I still had my doubts as we walked out the door. As we sat down at our seats I asked her, "Why did you agree with Kavana when she asked you?"

Bhoomija was convinced. "You heard her. It's one of the best modules. She said it's a *hot* skill—I'm sure that means something good, not bad."

"*Hot?*" Chetan abandoned his system and peeped into our desk separator. "I'll tell you what's hot. Your friend!"

Bhoomija and I exchanged looks. Wasn't it inappropriate for a middle-aged professional to call a colleague half his age *hot*, even for an eccentric nut-job like Chetan? I wanted to say something rude to him, but my brain froze—and suddenly I ran out of things to say. But, his mind was still running in the direction of my friend.

"What's her name?" he asked.

I continued to give him a guarded expression.

"Alisha," I said.

He repeated her name after me, nodded thoughtfully, and went back to whatever he was doing. Once he had plugged in his Beats on his system, and began to nod his head up and down to a Spanish song on the international radio, Bhoomija leaned closer to me and enquired if Alisha was in fact that attractive.

"She is beautiful," I said, shrugging my shoulders, "but I don't see why he's fussing over her that much."

I opened the Lync messenger and pinged Alisha, and a bunch of others to find out if CRM was as popular and in demand as Kavana had claimed it to be. Simultaneously, I searched for the same on Google.

The next day, Tarun arrived at half-past ten, flashed us his bright smile and enquired if we had booked a conference room for the *KT session.* Bhoomija flushed with embarrassment and cursed as if she had forgotten to do something she had been told to do. Tarun dismissed it with his hand and said never mind. He watered the plant on his desk with utmost devotion, gave us his toothy smile, and motioned us towards the conference rooms.

Fortunately, we found an empty conference room, and nobody claimed it during the *KT*. Tarun ran some PowerPoint slides—an old 2011 version that bore the initials

J. J., clearly not made by him—on the projector that we managed to get from another conference room where it was not being used.

Bhoomija wore a pink *kurti* with black *dhoti* pants and jangly earrings that made her look younger.

"I bought it from the *MAX* store," she said when I asked. "Went there with my roommate last night. How does it look?"

"It's pretty," I said. "You had time to go shopping after work?"

But then again, she stayed right around the bend from the office.

"Yes, why? What time do you reach home?"

"Nine thirty, if the traffic is kind," I replied.

"Why don't you note down what he's saying?"

We jumped at the voice. Kavana had stealthily entered the room and was standing behind us. We looked from one end of the table to the other, uncomfortably. We had left our bags on our desks and had no notebook with us. Kavana handed Bhoomija her own notebook and pen and asked her to note down, while I awkwardly pretended to help her with the noting down. I had a creepy feeling Kavana's eye never left us for the rest of the session. Post that, Bhoomija tried to impress Tarun by asking him various doubts and tried to strike a conversation.

We were free for the rest of the day. Bhoomija had packed food from her *paying guesthouse*, and I had mine from home, so we skipped the canteen and went to have lunch in the *break out area* instead. It was a small room at the back of the project area enclosed by a frosted glass door and suffused with such air conditioning that made you question yourself as to why you forgot to carry your Eskimo suit to the office this morning.

The idea behind it was obviously to frighten people into not taking breaks, or if they did, to drive them out of their break and send them scurrying back to the project area as quickly as possible. We plopped the two cold metal barstools in one corner where we figured the A.C hit least and opened our boxes. Bhoomija liked my mother's homemade *aloo paratha,* and I politely refused the rock hard *idlis* of her *paying guesthouse*. Her parents, she told me didn't approve of her plans of working for a corporate organization and living alone in the city. And she told me that apart from the food, living alone was the best decision she ever took. In fact, she sort of dreaded going home for the weekend. I looked at her incredulously.

"Well, for starters, I'll have to wake up at 6 A.M.," she whined, "the internet connectivity is bad, I won't be allowed to use my phone throughout the day, they'll dump chores on me, and then, at the end of it all I won't even be able to watch *F.R.I.E.N.D.S!*"

Bhoomija had discovered the 90s American sitcom recently as the television in her home had aired Telugu channels and a limited number of Hindi ones. Even if the channel was available her orthodox parents wouldn't permit her to watch an English show with risqué humour.

"Hey," I protested. "F.R.I.E.N.D.S so much more than that! It's like an era, a generation, a phase—"

"I know, I know, but my parents would never get it," she said, letting out a deep sigh. We finished our lunch and the room was getting unbearably cool now. We walked to the dusty old coffee machine on the counter.

"But, you know, parents are all the same in the city or village," I told her, reassuringly. I remembered my own experience of watching the show. I clicked the lemon tea button, but Bhoomija shook her head and told me none of the buttons work, except for coffee. "My parents didn't let me watch it either—in high school—I watched it anyway."

The machine poured more water than coffee. I took a sip and threw the rest in the sink when Bhoomija wasn't looking. Then, I got out of the walk-in freezer and took my seat beside Bhoomija in the project bay. My background research on CRM had yielded some results and I discussed it with her. It turned out that Kavana was not lying—CRM was one of the bustling fields in the current market, and trends showed that it would witness a growth in the coming years. What we didn't know was that we would be using such an outdated version of the application in *Popshake* that nobody in the current market would give us a job based on it.

It was *'fun Friday'*. The day where everyone wore jeans. And Chetan was no exception. But, as always he had gone a step ahead of everyone. He was wearing a pair of *Ray-Ban* shades inside the bay, and had also spiked his hair. Running a hand through it, he showed us a digital watch that he wore on his other hand. I wondered which kid he'd stolen it from.

At five in the evening, Chetan peeped into our desk and asked, "Why don't we go for a coffee?" Bhoomija and I exchanged a look. Never, in the one month that we had joined the project had he asked us for coffee.

Bhoomija responded delightedly, "Sure, Chetan."

We thought it was our ticket to knowing our project-mates better, even if it was one person. Absurd though he was, he could still be an entry. He knew quite a few people in the project. If we hung out with him, other people would see us and they would soon ask us to join them. Chetan snapped us out of our mastermind plan.

"By the way, call your friend as well," he said, winking at me. "*Aleeesha.*"

Apparently, he wouldn't give up on her. I had the unsettling feeling he was putting me in a spot. Nonetheless, I pinged Alisha. She was free and agreed to join us in the canteen.

"Good. I'll see you girls near the elevators," said Chetan, "I'll go now. You wait here for five minutes and then come out."

"You see, people *gossip,*" he said, lowering his voice. Then, he straightened up and walked to the front, without raising any suspicion.

The three of us met Alisha inside the canteen. We walked to the queue in front of the barista and waited for our turn.

"Half tea, or full?" asked Chetan, offering to pay. Bhoomija and I asked for half a glass of tea, each, while Alisha wanted a half coffee. Chetan repeated our order at the counter and passed the tiny glasses of steaming filter coffee and tea one by one. Then, he tore a sheet from his *Sodexo* meal-coupon passbook and placed it on the counter. The barista told him he needed a rupee more to clear the bill. Chetan shrugged. The man behind us in the queue was getting antsy.

"Anybody got a rupee?" Chetan asked us while he rummaged his battered wallet. "Ah, don't bother. Found it. *There you go.*"

It had begun to drizzle and the canteen was bustling with people. We found a table by the window overlooking the footpath, driveway and mini gardens. Alisha and I dusted some invisible dirt off the orange and green plastic chairs and sat down next to each other. Chetan took the seat opposite Alisha, and Bhoomija sat beside him.

"Aren't you going to introduce us?" Chetan asked me before I did, making me flush.

"I was going to— Chetan, Alisha. Alisha, Chetan—" I stuttered awkwardly.

"I'm Chetan," he said, confidently offering her his hand to shake. "I'm a manager. I've been working with Global for a year. Been in this industry for quite some time. I manage a team of six—two of them are here. If you can keep a secret—

" he leaned forward on the table and said with a wink, "I make twelve lakhs a year."

Alisha politely smiled. For the next fifteen minutes, Chetan gave her his undivided attention. He explained part of his work to her, asked her about her domain, complimented her on her looks, he even went on to say she looked like a particular Bollywood actress, *Jacqueline Fernandez*. Alisha flushed and shook her head. Bored, I looked out the window. It was raining heavily. Droplets of water continuously trickled down the glass and made the view blurry. Water logged on the footpath, and the streets glistened in the soft glow of the lampposts. An employee ran towards the building, covering his head in his hands. A few cars drove past. Dozens of employees were gathering by the windows.

"Nice weather," Bhoomija remarked. But Chetan ignored her. She rolled her eyes at me. I gave her a knowing look and stifled my yawn.

There was a sudden flash of lightning, and then a deafening thunder. The lampposts began to flicker. A second later, the canteen lights followed suit. One of the janitors began to draw the paper curtains oblivious of the crowd. People moved out in small groups. They would now go to the lobby to get a view of the rain. For somebody who stares at a computer screen all day, witnessing the rain is equivalent to watching the *aurora borealis* over the Arctic region.

Even Chetan had stopped talking. Once, the janitor pulled the curtain beside our table, Chetan looked to his tea that had turned cold. He gulped it in one go and pulled a face that showed how bad it tasted.

"So," he said, pushing the empty glass aside and rubbing his hands together on the table. "What are your future plans?"

"I'll work here for a few months. Once the bond period is complete I'm planning to pursue MSc. in the States," said Alisha. Until then, Alisha had answered only in monosyllables.

"Brilliant," said Chetan. "Why wait? Apply right away."

"No. I can't do that," she said. "I haven't taken the GREs."

My phone began to ring and suddenly they realized I was still on the same table. I looked at my phone and cut the call. A second later, it rang again. Bhoomija raised her eyebrow to ask me who it was. I shook my head to indicate that it was nobody important. I put my phone on silent and let it ring. At the same instant, Alisha took out her phone and put it to her ear.

"I have to take this," she told us and left the table.

I didn't hear her phone ring, but nobody else seemed to notice that. With no choice left, Chetan turned to us.

"How about your plans?" he asked. When both of us didn't answer, he went on, "You guys should do something. Go. Go to America, go to London. Leave this place."

"Why Chetan?" asked Bhoomija, immediately. "I like it here. I think Global Services is a nice company. I plan to work here and become a manager like you someday."

"And what would you get out of it?" Chetan shook his head vigorously. "I'll tell you it's all *fake. Pretense*," he said, enunciating the words slowly. "Look around you. Do you think anyone here is happy?"

I began to feel uncomfortable. What he was saying, I felt came from a place of negativity deep inside of him: midlife crises. I enjoyed the job, I told myself. Staring at the mailbox for hours was not a job, my mind retorted, but that was because the real job, 'productive work' as Kavana called it, hadn't begun. It would start soon as the CRM training was complete. Then, I'd work on something meaningful.

"It's a life-sucking machine," he went on. "What are you kids doing in a place like this?"

So, he did realize we were kids? I wanted to ask him what age he thought Alisha was.

"You should go out and carve a life for yourselves. Go, make history! Quit this job!" He thumped the table passionately. "All the things I would do if I were as young as you…"

I was being paid a salary, I quickly told myself. Yet, in the back of my mind, his words were playing their own game.

Chetan was studying me curiously. I shifted in my seat.

"You know how it is with silent folk?" he said, addressing me. "Their minds are always ticking. So, don't lie to me. What are you thinking?"

"Nothing."

I was feeling extremely uneasy. A thousand thoughts were running in my mind and I was glad he could read none of them.

"Come on," he challenged. "You can't be that boring!"

"I want to be a writer."

I said it before I could stop myself. My heart was racing faster than the speed of light. I had thought of it a couple of times but said it out loud for the first time. I exulted in the way the word sounded to my own ears.

"Yeah sure, and I want to be an *actor* in a French movie!" said Chetan, chuckling. "How can you have a dream like that all of a sudden?"

"It's not all of a sudden," I said, scornfully. I mentally counted. "Eleven years ago, I had the dream of becoming a writer. And I did write a story. Two actually."

"You wrote a story when you were *eleven?"* he repeated, as if he didn't believe me.

I was losing my patience.

"Yes. One at the age of ten. And, one at eleven along with a friend of mine," I said. "And it wasn't a two-page story or anything. It was a full-fledged novel of 200 pages!"

He laughed at me. And, asked me the question that could destroy an aspiring writer's dream.

"Did it get published?"

All the colour drained from my face, and I grimaced. *He didn't mean it as an insult,* I told myself, but my mind knew otherwise.

He continued to smirk at me. I kept my composure and answered coolly, "No, it didn't. But, we were called to the radio station for an interview about the story. *Radio City 14th November 2005."*

I was surprised I still remembered the date. But then, it was something I had done for my dreams, on my own, and I was proud of it. Bhoomija made a cheerful noise.

"Really?" she asked. I smiled at her. "Yes."

"*Ha*," Scoffed Chetan, stretching out his legs. "Anybody can write a story at ten… and go on a radio show. What have you done now? Stop blowing your own trumpet."

"I'm not—" I said through gritted teeth, and then thought better of it. I finally chose to shut up. There was no point in talking to him. I regretted having said anything. The rain had died down and the tube-lights glowed brightly in the empty canteen. Bhoomija too didn't say anything. A maid collected our empty glasses and gave it to the barista. The barista put them in the basin and closed the counter. We had been sitting there for an hour. From the passage beside the coffee shop, I saw Alisha coming towards us.

"*Ma chérie,* you are back," said Chetan, delightedly. I wanted to reach over the table and slap him.

Alisha's eyes widened for a second, then she pretended not to have heard it. "Listen, I came back to tell you I have to go," she said, without sitting down. "I have a lot of work."

I wanted a moment alone with Alisha, but Chetan got up to leave as well and all of us walked together to the elevators. When we reached our floor, Chetan walked to the project bay through the plastic archway in the centre and asked us to take a detour and come from the right side.

I locked my system and bade good-bye to Bhoomija. I wanted to go home and sleep for two days straight. But, the day wasn't over yet. A traffic jam awaited me outside the building, so bad that I was stuck for two hours, inside the tech park itself! As I sat there, amidst incessant honking and roaring of the wheels, I pondered over Chetan's words. Was I trying to find glory in a long lost achievement of mine? It had been forever since I wrote anything. Would I still be able to write? Did I still enjoy it? I unlocked my iPhone, clicked on the *Notes app* and decided to find out.

Five

First impressions don't always last. The one I had assumed to be a fairy godmother was actually a scheming, planning and gossiping wolf. And, I had a feeling she had begun to treat me differently.

Monday, we were back to the grind. I battled through another traffic jam in the morning and arrived half an hour late to the KT session. Kavana wrinkled her nose when I told her my excuse. Tarun brushed it off with a smile and gave me a recap of what he had presented until then.

"She isn't even supposed to be here till 11.30. What is her problem?" I whispered to Bhoomija when Kavana went out of the conference room to pick a call. "By the way, is that a new haircut?"

"Yes," she said, "I got it from the parlour in the mall last night. How do I look?"

Bhoomija had had her hair cut in layers. She moved her head from side to side to give me the complete view.

"Gorgeous," I said. "The fringe suits you."

It was not only the haircut, although that was the first thing one could notice, but also Bhoomija had undergone a complete makeover. Gone were her antique spectacles. She had purchased a pair of lenses. Modern, geometric bracelets replaced her glass bangles. Even her way of dressing had changed. Though she still wore traditional attire, she now bought colours that complimented her and *kurtis* that fit her well.

Kavana stormed inside and slumped on the chair opposite me.

"Guess who that was?" she said, addressing Tarun. He put the marker on the table and clapped his hands. "I don't know, tell me?"

"Amit," said Kavana, beaming and rolling her eyes. "He's buttering me up so much. I know he's dying for that onshore opportunity. He's literally offering to do my chores."

"Enjoy the royal treatment Kavana," Tarun said with a wink. "He wanted to go to Belgium, right? Is he?"

"Are you kidding me?" Kavana chuckled. "As long I'm in charge, he's not setting foot in Belgium, Netherlands or the United States."

"Come on, Kavana, forget the buttering. You know he's worked hard," pressed Tarun. " And, he's good at his job…Not only with the system but also with people. So, why not?"

"Good at their job or not, we *hate* our employees at *Popshake!"* said Kavana, chuckling. Then, to us, "Don't worry, you're safe. We don't hate employees with the lowest salary."

We chuckled uncomfortably.

"Besides, why are you so bothered? If you were given a choice, would you give up your onshore opportunity for Amit?" put in Kavana, slyly.

"Of course, not," retorted Tarun. "If it's CRM, I'm all for flying. And if not me—perhaps, you'll melt someday and let these girls fly."

Bhoomija and I smiled hesitantly.

"Don't put ideas into their head Tarun," said Kavana. "Give the presentation."

Tarun explained that the CRM application covered various areas such as Sales, Services, Marketing, Email, Customer

Support, Telesales et cetera. But in *Popshake,* we would be using only two areas of it: Sales and Services. He then gave out project-specific codes of the Sales feature.

"You're understanding everything, right?" asked Kavana, turning to Bhoomija. "Ask him if you have any doubts." She urged her to do so several times during the session, deliberately ignoring me.

Post the session, Bhoomija stayed back again to have a chat with Tarun, and I walked back to my seat alone. As I did, I saw a lot of heads turn. I looked down to see if there was something on my clothes, but no, I was fine. I ignored them and rushed to the safety of my computer screen. I opened the Lync messenger, and was about to ping Alisha, then decided against it. Chetan was on his desk and he would peep into mine any second. As if on cue, he gestured me to come to his system. A good weekend of sound sleep had dispelled my anger towards him. But, I still didn't have the mood to talk to him.

"Come here," he called again. Reluctantly, I maneuvered my chair to him. "Yes?" I asked. He pointed to his system. There was an MS Excel Spreadsheet opened on it. I didn't know what to make of it.

"You see that? That's my petrol reimbursement," he said. "I get paid Rs.4000/- each month for it. You should ask for it."

"Do you think they would give me?"

"They won't unless you ask for it. And in case they don't, you can ask for the office cabs at least." He opened another Spreadsheet. "See that?"

Bhoomija had come back then. She stood behind my chair and leaned on it to look at the screen.

"That's shift allowance," he said as he typed '1' on every cell in the box against his name. "By filling this I get an extra Rs.400/- every day for coming in the shift timing. Do you guys get it as well? Everybody here does."

I shook my head.

"I figured," he said, showing his typical smirk again. "You know whom to ask."

"Thanks, Chetan," said Bhoomija, "we will."

We went back to our seats to discuss the unfair treatment we were receiving in the project. And after we heard Kavana in the last meeting, we didn't trust her to be honest with us.

"I'll come with you. But it's best if you asked her," I whispered. "I don't think Kavana likes me."

No matter how much I tried to subdue it, it bothered me that Kavana didn't like me.

Bhoomija hesitated but didn't argue. "I think it's because you came late today."

"But there was so much traffic—" I retorted. "Anyway, I guess you're right. I'll come early tomorrow."

We walked to Kavana's desk, stealthily, rehearsing what Bhoomija would say to her.

Kavana raised an eyebrow when Bhoomija fumbled our query. Kavana's desk was right in the centre of *Popshake*, and I had a feeling everybody was watching us.

"Cabs, eh? I will get back to you about it," she said. "You can go to your desk."

Feeling accomplished, we went back. Later, when we ran into Kavana in the washroom, she broke our bubble.

"I'm sorry you won't be provided any cabs," she said, checking her reflection in the stained mirror. She adjusted the *dupatta* of her gaudy *salwar suit*. "Cabs are for people who come in the shift timings."

"We could come in the shift timing," said Bhoomija, straightaway.

"Ah, you see… that won't be necessary."

"K—Kavana," I said, timidly. "Can we get petrol reimbursement—"

"That's only for managers," she said and slammed the door behind her.

"So we'll neither be given shift allowance nor cabs—and petrol is out of the question." I fretted, imitating her squeaky voice, *"That's only for managers."*

Bhoomija shushed me. "Someone might hear you."

I met Alisha for lunch. Bhoomija refused to come down to the canteen. She told me she had brought a lunch box and wanted to eat in the *break out area.* I had a hunch she wanted to accompany Tarun, so I left her alone.

Alisha took a call when we came down from the elevator and strode past the lobby. *Three guesses who?* But, to my great relief, she told him that she was with a friend—me—and that she would ring him afterward.

The canteen was packed with people and carried a heavy, pungent odour of food and sweat. Perhaps a major culprit was the *Dosa* counter that created clouds of steam and had no exhaust. Alisha bought a *set dosa* from there.

"After what happened last time, I didn't think you would meet me again," I said, taking a bite of my soggy *chapatti* with homemade *daal*. "I didn't know Chetan would behave like that. I swear."

"That was not your fault," she said, dispelling my guilt. "What an *ass!* He's so old. I can't believe he is like that. I'm sure he has a wife."

"A very pretty wife," I corrected her.

"Great! Guess what?" she exclaimed. "He found on me on *Lync* today and asked me out on a date."

My eyes popped out of my sockets.

"And?"

"Obviously, I don't want to go," said Alisha, offended. "But, I gave him a vague answer. I told him I'd check my schedule because I wanted to speak to you first. I didn't want to be rude. After all, he is your colleague."

I considered what she said for a moment. I took a swig of water from my bottle to wash down my *chapatti*. Homemade food was good as long it as was hot. I planned to eat *chapattis* for breakfast from then on, and bring something dry to the office.

Chetan was stepping way out of line. But, the answer was simple.

"That's right," I said, "He is *my* colleague. Not yours. Be as rude as you want to be."

Alisha chuckled. " Super."

My phone rang, and I cut the call.

"You never pick anyone's call, do you?"

I gave her a guilty smile and lied. "My signal is bad in the canteen area."

"Yes, this is like the basement. Terrible network. That reminds me I have to call Dee before going back," she said. "Why don't we go for a walk outside and I can call him?"

I shrugged. "Sure."

First, we made sure nobody from our team was around, especially Kavana. Alisha was lucky that way. Her team lead was on vacation for her wedding and connected remotely from her home in Delhi. Next, we swiped our access cards at the back door of the canteen and got out into the fresh air. It's not that nobody went for a walk outside the office post-lunch. Everybody did. It wouldn't turn into a big deal unless you were spotted.

The air didn't remain fresh for long. As we took a few steps outside the building an overpowering smell of human faeces and urine engulfed us, making us want to barf. I closed my nose and mouth tightly and Alisha coughed on the call. We ran as fast as we could, crossing four buildings, but the stench followed us.

"Quick, here!" I said, spotting a tree-covered region to my left.

We sat on the kerb under a berry tree, escaping the scorching sun in its shade. I was grateful the smell didn't catch up. Underneath us was another company's parking lot. Now and then a car would pull out, making the ground below us reverberate. I could no longer see Global Services employees. I was glad.

"No, I can't," said Alisha, blushing into her phone. "I'm with Sanchita—she's right here…"

I wished I wasn't. I gave her a pasted smile to act as if I didn't understand what was happening from the one-side conversation I was hearing.

Deepak and I went to the same school, and much as I didn't like him, I knew it wouldn't hurt to say a *hello*. Moreover, Alisha was my friend now. So I did. We spoke for 20 seconds and I handed the phone back to her.

"I'm so glad you like Dee," said Alisha, after she ended the call. "My other friends detest him for some reason. And I can never talk to them about him…He's not bad you know."

I nodded and kept my opinions to myself.

Meanwhile, a security guard of another office shooed us from the kerb. We took a turn and went through the front doors of Global Services, up the elevators and to our respective floors. Kavana was back when I came in, and eyed me suspiciously. Lately, she had developed hawk eyes that followed me everywhere. Bhoomija was in an exceptionally good mood when I came to my seat.

"So, what is going on with you two?" I teased her, eyeing Tarun's desk.

"Actually, we are going to the movies this Friday," she said.

"He asked you out?"

"Actually, I asked him," said Bhoomija, blushing. "He was telling me his friends watched Captain America without him. So, I asked him if he wanted to go with me. And he said yes."

"Bingo," I winked at her.

"He showed me pictures of his family home in Kerala," she went on. "It's so big. He's even got a swimming pool inside his house. No wonder he's so fit. I should probably start going to the gym too. Have I put on weight?"

"No," I said. "Maybe a little."

In the evening, Tarun accompanied Bhoomija and me for a cup of coffee. Whom should we run into, but Kavana? She was shocked to see the three of us together and she made no secret of it.

We didn't have any work that day after we came back, and we waited for the clock to hit seven-thirty. It hadn't rained, and I easily crossed the tech park. But there was a huge traffic jam above the Bellandur flyover. I took out my cellphone and once again hit the *Notes app* while listening to Hindi music in the background.

This time, I wrote a short story based on the day's happenings—*A girl waiting to go on her first date. It didn't end well in my story.* I called it—'Traffic Time Story', based on its place of origin. I opened *Facebook* to upload the story; I wanted to know what my friends thought of it. Then I decided I was not ready for it and closed the social media page.

The next morning, I hurried through my activities and reached the office on time. I ran to swipe my card at the fifth-floor entrance because until I did that, my presence in the office didn't count. We had to charge in 10 hours every day, mandatorily, despite numerous health surveys that strictly advised offices not to work their employees more than 8 hours a day, which put them at serious health risks. The additional 3 hours that one spent in traffic daily was nobody's concern.

Bhoomija was on the way to the conference room when I caught a glimpse of her. I didn't put my bag on my desk; instead, I carried it with me and dashed in the direction she went. Tarun was nowhere to be seen. Fifteen minutes later, Kavana came to tell us that the KT session wouldn't happen that day as Tarun was on sick leave.

"Great," I sighed.

But, Kavana was in a worse mood than me that morning. "Why can't he keep me informed? So irresponsible. I'm sick of that guy." She thumped her laptop on the desk. She saw the manager pass by and quickly ducked out to call him.

"I think it's time we remove Tarun from the project," she told him as soon as he entered the room. "The guy is extremely irresponsible. Lazy. Uninterested. We're getting nothing out of him anymore."

Bhoomija and I exchanged a look. I felt something in the pit of my stomach. Tarun was Kavana's number one confidante.

"Are you out of your senses Kavana?" he asked sharply. The manager was a tall man in a clean white shirt and had a goatee that gave his face a funny twist. "I won't have anyone for CRM if I remove him. He is single-handedly managing that module from 3 years."

Kavana flushed with embarrassment. "Err… about that… I have found two replacements for Tarun."

We gulped and looked at each other. "Bhoomija and Sanchita."

"You want me to give the entire module to juniors?" he barked.

"They're brilliant. They've learnt everything from Tarun. Together they can definitely manage the module," urged Kavana. "Besides, I will be there to watch over them. I can handle it if they face any problems."

The manager chuckled. "Kavana, if you knew CRM I would've removed Tarun long ago."

"Vishal!" said Kavana, and looked at us from the corner of her beetle eyes.

The manager looked at us as well, and I sincerely hoped I was maintaining an impassive face.

He let out a sigh. "Fine. I'll consider your request. We'll discuss it later."

"Thank you, Vishal."

Kavana was jubilant. "You both, listen to me," she said after he left. "None of what happened here goes out of this room. Okay?"

We nodded.

"Can I count on you two to be ready by next week? Learn everything from him. Don't leave anything out."

I felt like a ticking bomb had been attached to me. Bhoomija and I knew nothing of value in CRM that would be used in our project. Most of Tarun's presentations were vague and went over our heads. The concepts we managed to grasp in them were too generic, and would perhaps never come to practical use. One week was too short a period to suddenly understand the whole module. But, we were afraid to say it to Kavana, so we just nodded.

"And, not a word to Tarun!" she warned, "Girls, as soon as you learn the module from him, he's out. So don't go mingling with him everywhere."

"You can leave now, I'll send you some CRM documents and you can study from them today."

As promised, Kavana mailed a few CRM documents to Bhoomija's email id. *Only* to her email id. I felt it unnecessary to take it up with Kavana, as Bhoomija readily forwarded the mails to me.

Bhoomija and I agreed not to disclose the information to Tarun, albeit it was unfair. We wanted to remain in Kavana's good books.

On the other hand, Alisha was behaving strangely. She didn't ping me on Lync, although she was online from the morning. She even refused to meet me for lunch.

Two days later, she pinged me one evening.

"Can you meet me for a quick coffee?" she asked. "NOW."

"Sure," I said. "I'll be there in 2 minutes."

"What's up?" I asked, sitting across the table from her in one corner. She wanted to skip the line at the common coffee counter, so we went to *au Bon Pain* café instead. Also, one of her colleagues had warned her that the barista didn't wash the glasses properly, so she preferred the paper cups at *au Bon Pain* café.

"My team lead is back," said Alisha, taking a sip of her hot cappuccino. "And she's making my life hell."

"I thought she liked you." Blowing over my coffee, I cautiously sipped it. It was too bitter for my taste, so I poured a second packet of white sugar in it and stirred.

"She did. I don't know what happened. She liked my work and had approved everything from Delhi. Now, all of a sudden, she wants me to change the whole report. It took me a month to make it," she said.

"Shit."

"It's not just that, she sits right next to me and starts yelling at me if I take a break for more than ten minutes, even for lunch. She constantly peeps into my computer. For god's sake, she keeps count of the times I go to pee!"

I laughed despite myself. "Crazy!"

"Need to get back before she does. I'm so sick of her. I don't know why she hates me."

"Well, if it's any consolation, my lead hates me too," I said, toying the stirring stick.

"What did she do?" Alisha gulped the last of her coffee and set the paper cup down. "Ah, that feels so much better. My head isn't aching that badly."

I am not a coffee person, and I can never relate to that emotion. I was developing a stomachache thanks to the bitter coffee. No amount of sugar could make it better.

"Perhaps, I'm imagining it," I said, shrugging my shoulders. "She is so nice to Bhoomija, but when she speaks to me she becomes cynical. Like I'm hiding some secret weapon and she knows about it."

Alisha laughed.

"When it comes to project-related stuff—meetings or documents—she only tells Bhoomija. And I have to take it from her. I don't understand. I never did anything to piss her off."

"That's unfair. Stand up for your rights, man. Ask her."

"I can't," I said, shaking my head.

Alisha cursed and quickly ducked under the table.

I instantly turned around.

"That's *her.*"

"That's your team lead?" I asked disbelievingly.

She was the polar opposite of what I had imagined. She looked like the stem of a dead plant: skinny, sullen and lifeless. And her clothes looked like a gunny bag, thrown over her shoulders. And the fact that they were brown in color didn't help.

"She had gone to speak to the manager, so I came downstairs. I'm so dead," Alisha spoke, in hushed tones.

"Relax, *she* didn't see you."

"Oh my god, that's my manager," Alisha exclaimed. "What are they doing together?"

"She never gets out of the project bay," said Alisha, still following them with her eyes. We saw them walk to the coffee counter and join the queue in front. Then, Alisha relaxed.

For a while, we sat in silence, pondering over our '*team lead situation*', breathing-in the scent of pastries and resisting the urge to eat one. Alisha was eyeing me keenly.

She raised an eyebrow at me, inquisitively.

"I may have a solution to your problem," I said. "You need to lose the make-up."

"Lose the watch!" she told me instantly.

We gaped at each other and burst out laughing.

"Honestly, you think that's the problem?" I asked, standing at the counter. We had finally caved in and were buying some chocolate chip cookies.

"You're wearing a *Tissot*!"

Alisha took the tray of cookies to our table and we settled in.

"Do you really think my lead is jealous of *me*?" she asked.

"Have you seen her? She looks like a zombie."

"She does, doesn't she? That bitch—making my life hard," cursed Alisha, her mouth full with a big chunk of cookie.

"Maybe you should wear rags too."

"Agreed. I'll wear rubbish from tomorrow," said Alisha. "Let's do this."

"Mission-Ugly-and-Poor." We fist-bumped to it.

We were so excited to have found some key that it didn't occur to us how bizarre it was. We only wanted to fit in and be accepted. Alisha wanted to go back before her team lead. So we put our paper cups in the bin, placed the tray on the used counter and left. I pushed my watch into the sleeve of my shirt as we walked back to the elevators, discussing the elaborate details of our plan on the way.

"If anybody asks you about your imported bracelets—"

"I bought it from a street vendor in Jayanagar."

"Perfect."

My cellphone began to ring. I jumped and fumbled for it in my pocket. We were still in the elevator.

"And, you complain that your network is bad?" Alisha was looking at me disbelievingly.

I saw the name and cut the call. Why did he have to call me at the wrong time, always? I turned on the silent mode and put it in my pocket. I caught Alisha looking at me, shrewdly.

"Do you want to tell me who Raghav is?"

I looked from her to the sliding doors. I licked my dry lips and sighed. "He's my boyfriend." I watched the other people in the lift as I said it. Thankfully, I knew none of them.

"You never told me you had a boyfriend," exclaimed Alisha, poking my waist.

"There wasn't much to say."

The doors of the elevator opened on my floor.

"You're not getting away that easy." Alisha held my hand tightly.

I tried to get out of her grip. Meanwhile, two others got out of the elevators on the same floor. "How? When? For how long?"

Everybody in the lift was watching us. I struggled out of her grip and went out of the elevator. She stood at the door of the lift; she wanted to come after me. At that instant, the elevator opposite us opened. Alisha's team lead and manager were on it.

"Are you getting out or I'll close the doors?" barked someone agitatedly, hitting the button on the pad.

I pushed Alisha inside the lift and she reluctantly went up.

Six

As soon as I sat down on my seat, Alisha's *Lync* status went from 'Away' to 'Available.' I thought I saw a few people stare at me on my way back, but in a room full of people gazing at their computers, anyone who was not doing the same could hardly go unnoticed.

ALISHA: What the hell?

ME: Hi

ALISHA: HI YOURSELF!

When were you going to tell me about your boyfriend?

ME: Actually, never.

I typed, which was partly true.

ALISHA: DA FUCK!

ME: Ha ha. Okay. I'm sorry. I should have told you earlier.

PS- I don't think you should say f*ck on the office computer. It might be tracked.

ALISHA: FUCK FUCK FUCK

ME: Okay. Miss Rebel. How wise!

ALISHA: Don't go off-topic. Tell me the whole story.

PS- Emails that are tracked. As long as we're on messenger, we're safe.

ME: There isn't any '*story*' to tell you.

It was a spur of the moment kind of thing. He asked, and I said yes.

PS- If you say so.

ALISHA: Spur of the moment. Ooooh. That's romantic. Continue.

PS- Also, putting an asterisk in fuck won't stop it from getting tracked. FYI.

ME: Guess I brought that on myself. Wrong usage of words. *(Face-palm)*

PS- would you stop saying fuck already? Yes, you read that right. I give up trying to be good on messenger.

ALISHA: Fuck. My team lead peeped into my computer.

Then, an array of unintelligible characters followed making our real messages scroll up.

ALISHA: We're not done here. *BRB.*

I closed the chatbox to delete the messages. Then, I locked my computer and went to the break out area. Bhoomija went to the washroom before leaving.

I thought about it for a moment and took out my cellphone.

"Hello beautiful," answered Raghav on the third ring.

I drew in a sharp breath.

"How is the evening treating you?"

"Badly," I snapped. "Listen, I have told you so many times not to call me when I'm in the office."

"Sorry. I thought you might be in your car."

"No. My shift gets done at seven-thirty. And I still have twenty minutes to go. Anyway, why did you call me?"

"I wanted to know if you liked pink more than lavender?" He said, and a second later realized his error. "But—you sound awfully frustrated. What's the trouble?"

"Neither. I like black, okay?" I snapped.

"Look, I'm sorry. I know it's not your fault," I went on. "I have some issues at the office, and now isn't a good time to discuss favourite colours."

"I hear you. What is troubling you so much?" he drawled. "I could be your genie."

"So if I told you my troubles you could make them disappear?" I mocked.

"Try me."

He was being so nice to me. I felt guilty and decided to share my thoughts with him.

"I have a feeling my team lead dislikes me. Highly dislikes me," I said. "And my friend says it's because I'm rich. I'm trying to get into her good books."

"Hmm…" He contemplated it. "One way to impress the boss is to be around them all the time. Go with her to lunch. Tea. Ask her about her day, family, favourite food, work. Do small chores for her…"

"Isn't that—"

"Kiss ass?" he went on. "It is. But, everybody does it."

"Isn't it enough that I'm good at my work?" I was so agitated at this point that I wanted to pull my hair. Suddenly, the glass door creaked and Kavana entered.

I gulped. My throat went dry. Raghav said something on the phone but I wasn't listening. I put the phone down from my ear, but she had seen it.

"Hi Kavana," I said, still holding the phone in my hand but hiding the screen from her.

She went to get a glass of water, completely ignoring me. The temperature in the room had turned from cold to chilly, and the air conditioning had little to do with it.

"How many friends do you have here?" It was more of a statement than a question.

"You're either going to the canteen with them or talking on the phone. Have you finished your work? Did you read those documents I sent you?"

"Yes Kavana, I read them. I sent the mail you had asked, to the security team to get access to the client systems."

"I know," she said, set her glass down, and walked out.

Shit. The damage was done.

Sighing, I put my phone in the pocket and walked to my desk. My head held low, I dragged my feet, one in front of the other putting as much distance as I could between Kavana and me. Raghav had cut the call. Bhoomija could tell from my face that something was wrong, she raised an eyebrow, but I shook my head.

"Let's go or I'll miss my bus," Bhoomija urged me.

At 7.25 P.M we locked our systems, and ran out of the project bay, drawing jealous stares of others whose shift had not yet ended. Once we got into the elevator, Bhoomija was relieved.

"It's Friday tomorrow," she shook my arm, excitedly. The lift was empty. "What do you think I should wear?"

"Why don't you wear your pink kurti with black bottoms?" I asked, matching her enthusiasm.

"Thanks. And, how are these earrings?" she showed me a picture of a pair of small *jhoomkis* on her phone. I told her they were fabulous. The elevator doors opened on the ground floor and we walked fast across the lobby and reception, towards the exit. Bhoomija dragged my arm and stopped me.

"He'll show up tomorrow, right?"

"He will," I said.

She gave me an unexpected hug and left.

On my way home that evening, I wrote a fantasy tale about a monster boss, who undoubtedly resembled mine, who consumed her employees for supper every fortnight. I called it Traffic Time Story 2, again based on where I was when I wrote it. I was in such a delighted mood after that, that I didn't mind the double traffic jams I faced at Koramangala and Dairy Circle.

On Friday, my doubts were confirmed. Bhoomija pulled me by the sleeve and took me to the break out area when I came to my desk. Bhoomija had been restless until Tarun had shown up that morning. I had skipped my breakfast in order to come early to office and had gone for a bite to the canteen after the KT session.

"What?" I asked her, folding my arms for warmth. There was someone in the break out area and she waited for him to walk out.

"Did you tell Kavana you come to the office in an *Innova*?"

"No," I said. "I never told anyone."

Bhoomija looked at me skeptically, "Kavana came to the desk after KT and she asked me, '*Is this how rich girls behave?*' looking at your seat. I told her you had gone to the washroom. I didn't tell her you went to the canteen. But, she said—'*She comes in a chauffeur-driven car. Why can't she come early?*'"

"I did come early," I protested loudly. "It was just one time that I came late. She can't hold that against me forever."

"I told her you have been coming early," said Bhoomija.

"How did she know about my car?"

"Did you tell anyone else here, apart from me, that you travel by car?"

I thought about it for a minute. I hadn't told anyone about it. I saw my car as a means of transportation, but after my discussion with Alisha, I figured the others wouldn't see it that way. So I had been asking my driver to stop a little distance away from the office building.

"No, I haven't," I said. Suddenly I remembered something that had happened the previous week. "But..."

"But?"

"Chetan saw me climb into my car last Friday," I said. "I didn't think it meant anything."

Bhoomija gaped at me. "If Chetan knows, the whole office knows."

On one of his evening walks around the building last Friday, Chetan had stopped directly in front of my car and had stared inside.

"That is why people have been staring at me all this time?"

Bhoomija nodded. "You can't go back and change it. Anyway, be careful with Kavana. Let's go back, or she'll be mad again."

Mission-Ugly-and-Poor failed before its inception on my end. I wondered how it was going for Alisha. Her *Lync* status was 'Do not disturb' from the morning. Meanwhile, I saw Chetan sitting on his seat beside Bhoomija. He had his Beats headphones on, tuned in to an international radio station, and was bobbing his head from side to side. The very sight of him pissed me off.

Bhoomija avoided Tarun for lunch fearing Kavana and joined Alisha and me. Alisha wore a shabby top and an old pair of flannels. Her caramel hair was tied at the back with a band and didn't have the alluring effect it normally did when it fell on her shoulders. She wore no makeup. Bhoomija asked her if she was unwell. Alisha and I exchanged secret smiles. Our plan was in place. Alisha assured Bhoomija she was fine. But, when she refused to have lunch and opted for a glass of orange juice, I wondered if she was in fact, unwell. Her eyes, I noted then, did look sunken.

"Are you all right?" I asked her, pointing to the juice in her hand.

"I'm fine," she said. "Don't have the appetite. Slept badly last night. Random fight with my boyfriend."

When I asked her what it was about, she dismissed the topic. I didn't want to pry, so I dropped it. The call she awaited came when we were sitting under the berry tree after lunch. After speaking to her boyfriend Alisha's spirits lifted.

Kavana had sent us a message on *Lync* by the time we went back upstairs. She wanted to see us at her desk *A.S.A.P.*

"How long do you girls take to have lunch?" she asked as soon as we went to her.

We shuffled our feet and didn't answer. And Kavana continued to humiliate us. "Don't think that people are not watching you. The manager knows everything."

"We went for half an hour, *Kavana*," said Bhoomija, raising her voice. Kavana stared in amazement. The whole bay was now watching us silently. Therefore, Kavana shifted gears. "Anyway—I called you here to tell you this. I want you ready by next week," then she lowered her voice and asked us to lean in, "I'm preponing Tarun's last date. Stop using Tarun's credentials to login to the client system and start using your own."

"But—Kavana one week is not enough—," Bhoomija prompted.

"I don't want your excuses," Kavana held up her hand. "Next week is final. It's not your decision." We nodded and left.

"This is so unfair," Bhoomija whispered to me as we went back to our desks.

"I know. Tarun is our mentor. He's one of those mentors who actually taught us something." It had been running on my mind since the meeting with Vishal, our manager. It was like learning the subject and kicking your teacher out. Maybe, I'm exaggerating, and maybe it was common in IT, but in the eyes of two Associate Software Engineers fresh out of college and barely surviving two months in office: it was ruthless.

Firstly, because it was taking place in discreet. And secondly, because it meant that we could be sacked in the same manner.

"I can't believe I won't be seeing Tarun in our bay from next week," said Bhoomija.

"I can't believe they're dumping the whole module on us. We don't know anything, practically," I said.

"What do we do?"

I shrugged. Tarun spun on us in his gleeful manner. "Where did you go? I was looking for you," he said to Bhoomija. He offered us a peppermint, each. He put his empty lunch box in his bag and switched on his laptop.

"I—I went with Sanchi," Bhoomija flushed like the colour of her *kurti*.

"Never mind," he said, giving her one of his disarming smiles. He got up from his desk and came to ours. He pulled up a chair and sat beside Bhoomija. "We can go for coffee, later."

"Why don't you join us too, Sanchi?" he asked me. I nodded in agreement. Then he showed us the tasks to do on the client system. "Check these tasks, as soon as you come, every day. If you find any discrepancies go to the coding team and have them re-run the program. You can divide it between yourselves. It's up to you. But, do it before I come to the office."

I looked at Bhoomija, but she was watching the screen with paramount concentration. If Tarun knew he was going to be fired, from the project or perhaps from the company, and we were his replacements, would he still want to teach us?

"Are we clear?" asked Tarun, bringing me out of my thoughts. I nodded. "Good. Now, I'll show you how to fix the error if the client logs a complaint in our system."

"Categorize the error. You can tally it against the documentation. Ninety percent of the time it will fall broadly under these seven types," he pointed to a list. "Once you find a match, all you have to do is follow the step by step procedure I have laid out for each type. Let me give you an example..."

"What if it doesn't match the seven types?" I asked after he showed us a sample error. I was chewing a piece of gum to stifle my yawn. An hour had passed since Tarun had started the hands-on presentation.

Tarun turned to me and took a deep breath. "The procedure is simple—you'll have to get inside the customized code, dismantle each one to find out what exactly caused the error. It could take from hours—to years depending on your luck. In other words: You. Are. Screwed." He gave me a slow lop-sided smile. Bhoomija and I exchanged a glance.

"But, if at all that happens you have me, Google and the coding team," Tarun reassured. Then, he pushed the keyboard and yawned. "That's enough learning for one day. Come on, let's go for a break."

I gazed across the room. Kavana was on her desk, two rows ahead of us. So I told Tarun that Bhoomija and I would join him at the elevators.

We didn't want to arouse Kavana's suspicion further, so Bhoomija and I took a detour to the washroom and joined Tarun at the elevators. We munched on *bhel puri*, *peanut chaat,* and *samosas* along with our evening tea.

"Shall we book the tickets online?" asked Bhoomija, taking a large scoop of the *peanut chaat.*

"Sorry?"

"For Captain America."

"Right… I'm so sorry, I forgot," said Tarun. "My shift gets over at nine today. But I have an important meeting after that."

Bhoomija gulped and scowled at him. I pretended like I didn't know about their plans.

"It's okay," she said, finally.

I felt sorry for Bhoomija. She had been preparing for it for days, bombarding me with queries about her attire, accessories, topics to speak with him, and the kind of food she must order.

"Let me see what I can do," said Tarun, taking out his cellphone. Dialing someone, he excused himself from the table and walked back and forth at the coffee counter.

"How could he forget?"

I wrinkled my nose in distaste and shook my head.

Tarun returned to our table and clapped his hands. "Alright, let's go to that movie tonight," he winked at Bhoomija.

"What about your meeting?"

"Postponed it."

There was no stopping Bhoomija now. She was beaming.

"Yes, he forgot. But then, he canceled his *important* meeting for me. That means something, right?" she asked me on the elevator when I was leaving.

"Definitely."

Bhoomija planned to stay back and hide in the canteen till Tarun finished his shift.

"I've never been out at this time of the night," said Bhoomija. The movie was at nine forty in *Central Mall.* "My parents would be furious if they knew."

"Don't worry, you'll love it," I said, looking up at the sky outside the building. The evening was blessed with clear skies, twinkling stars, and weather we referred to as *typical Bangalore weather:* neither too cold, nor too warm—just right.

Seven

Monday, Bhoomija told me she had had a great night. Tarun dropped her to the paying guesthouse after the movie on Friday. But the gate was locked, and the compound was too high for her to jump—although she did give it a try—hence, they stayed out the whole night. They rode to the Bangalore International Airport on his bike and had a cup of coffee and midnight snacks, and watched the sun come up.

My weekend was eventful as well. I met Nishant for a couple of drinks at a resto-bar in Koramangala and we whined about how we could not bunk office on our whims, like the college lectures that we used to. He teased me about my weight. I don't feel I gained any, maybe a kilogram or two. On the other hand, he looked significantly thinner than usual. I asked him if he was smoking pot again, but he denied it.

Bhoomija was successful in dodging her parents' call on Friday. They had called her at night while she was in the cinema theatre. But she was not quite effective in hiding Kavana's plan from Tarun. Somewhere in the quiet hours of the night, except for the occasional hum and roar of flights taking off, that time when everybody spills their secrets, she told him.

It came to him as a shock. He was angry for a while and then, she told me, he became stoically calm. In knowing the secret, he had gained the upper hand. He thanked Bhoomija for telling him. He could now bandage the wound before it cut deeper. He intended to stay in the company and the project until he found something better, and he told her he would pull some strings with the senior manager, Vishal's supervisor. It seems both of them had something in common, their hometown.

I was neither surprised nor upset. I knew she would tell him; it was a matter of time. Besides, if she hadn't told him I know I would.

Chetan came in at mid-day. And, the first thing he did was make fun of Bhoomija's hair. She had tied it into a braid. He mocked that she looked like his maid. Bhoomija was angry, but she didn't have a comeback, so she kept quiet.

"Ignore him," I told her.

"My mother found out I cut my hair."

"Was it bad?" I asked her. Bhoomija had told me it was considered blasphemous in her village if a woman cut her hair post-puberty.

"She chased me," said Bhoomija. "With a rolling pin!"

"Crap," I laughed despite myself.

"This morning she oiled my hair and braided it before I boarded the bus," she said.

"Do I look disgusting?" she asked, checking her reflection on the black screen of her phone and scowling. "Nobody spoke to me from morning. Chetan's right, nobody braids their hair to office."

"I braid my hair sometimes," I told her, reassuringly. But, she went to the washroom, undid her braid and tied her greasy hair into a ponytail.

Tarun treated Bhoomija and me ordinarily. But, he was struggling to keep his façade in front of Kavana. He was either too sugary or too insolent. I was afraid Kavana might make a guess. Bhoomija assured me that our names would not come up even if she did find out.

I took Raghav's advice of talking to each one separately. When I met a team member in the washroom, I quickly struck up a conversation. It didn't last more than thirty seconds. Then, a repeat episode of it happened in the canteen with another colleague. Alisha had no luck either. The more work she completed, the more her team lead criticized it and sent it back for rework. Meanwhile, Alisha's colleague enjoyed all the credits.

"I want to mess it up on purpose and make him get screwed for it."

I chuckled. "Relax. Forget office issues. How's Dee?"

"He's good," she said, cheering up instantly. "He's coming to pick me up today. We're having a house party."

"Hey, why don't you come too?" she asked.

"Err… No, thanks." I said, awkwardly. "You carry on. I have some work—"

"Come don't be shy," Alisha insisted, leaning forward on the coffee table of au Bon Pain. I didn't like parties, and I didn't like strangers, and I had a feeling she was inviting me out of formality.

"I have some work. Besides, I don't even know anyone there."

"A couple of our college mates are coming," she said "some friends of Dee. It's a mixed crowd. I don't know half of them either. Trust me."

She persisted until I agreed.

I told my family I would be staying at my friend's place. Alisha had one roommate and she said we could manage. Dee arrived in a blue Honda Brio to pick us up at seven. I noticed the paint chipping off in places and a dent near the door as I got into the backseat. The inside of his car was unkempt and smelled of liquor and smoke. I pushed the beer carton aside and sat down.

"Hi Deepak," I said, as he drove out of the tech park and onto the main road.

"Sanchi," he yelled, over the blaring music he was playing. "Man, I didn't know you partied."

He smirked at me from the rearview mirror. Lo and behold, he was getting on my nerves even before the party started. I gave him a pasted smile and didn't bother answering.

As I feared, it was a ride in the death cab. He drove at the speed of 100kmph in peak hour traffic, hitting the brake and accelerator alternatively. We almost dashed a bike, two auto-rickshaws, and a pedestrian before getting onto the Marathahalli flyover.

"DEE," yelled Alisha. "What are you doing? Are you drunk?"

Deepak hit the brake in the last moment to avoid dashing a bus. I fell forward in the seat and the beer carton fell into my lap.

"Shut up Ali," He changed the gears, and grunted seeing the traffic on the flyover. "Just had a beer to warm up. I'm not drunk."

I pushed the carton aside. I was glad when the ride came to an end in front of Alisha's apartment in an alley below the flyover. Alisha lived on the third floor in a spacious two-bedroom apartment with a hall, kitchen, and bathroom. The balcony overlooked a large swimming pool and front lawns. Deepak parked his car in the visitor's parking area in the basement and joined us upstairs. Alisha's roommate, Radhika, had let some friends in and the party had begun. His buddies slapped him on the back and took the carton from him. I awkwardly greeted them as Alisha introduced me, but forgot their names instantly.

Radhika was plump, had a bob cut, and was dressed in a floor-length gown. She had invited two of her friends—tall, skinny girls dressed in crop tops and leather mini skirts. Alisha told me she had met them on a few occasions earlier, but didn't like them much. Four of Deepak's male friends from college and two from work had come.

Alisha went to change into a shimmering dress that she had bought from an online store. I was still in my cotton slacks from work. She offered to lend me her party wear, but I refused. By the time Alisha came out, Deepak was deep in conversation with one of the leather skirt girls. Alisha pretended not to notice and sat on the sofa beside me. He was narrating one of his hiking trip stories, one where he had found a rare intoxicant in a secluded village below the Himalayas. The girl seemed to be impressed. Deepak ran a hand through his hair and leaned forward.

"Now, why do I have a feeling your intoxicant is fermented potato?" he asked, reaching out. "You're a vodka girl!"

"How did you know?" she said, taking his hand.

"Come on, let me make you a shot." He got up from his chair and led her into the kitchen.

"Dee, get us all some nachos from there," Alisha barked after him. Deepak waved his hand in the air to show he had heard her. Then, Alisha played music so loud that nobody could have a decent conversation anymore. Satisfied, she poured herself some rum and coke. I grabbed a beer. The Bluetooth speaker played Katy Perry's 'Chained To The Rhythm.'

I gave Alisha a knowing smile because it was one of our favourite songs. It somewhat reminded me of my situation. I had these occasional bursts of passion for writing, but mostly I was stuck in a multinational company pursuing a career in engineering, living my life in a loop, like everybody else, like the giant hamster wheel Katy Perry runs on in the music video.

The doorbell rang and took me out of my contemplation. Radhika went to the door and carried the pizzas and chop suey noodles that we had ordered. Deepak and the girl had come out of the kitchen with a couple of vodka bottles. We dug into the pizzas, played the board game Monopoly and drank some shots, up to a point where nobody knew what was happening in the game anymore and then we pushed it aside. Radhika covered her mouth and ran to the bathroom. I was feeling hot and I went to the balcony for some fresh air. Alisha was dancing with a former college buddy. Two of Deepak's friends went to take a dip in the pool. I could see them from the balcony. They only took off their shoes and got into the water. I wondered if they knew they didn't have anything else to change into. But, they weren't the stupidest. One of the leather skirt girls hit it off with Deepak's colleague and both of them ran down the stairs to the pool. And suddenly, instead of dipping into the pool, they began practicing yoga in front of it. I burst out laughing. Deepak and the other girl joined in my laughter from the adjacent balcony. That's when it happened.

Suddenly, we heard Alisha scream. The three of us ran back inside.

"Duuuude!" she was screaming at Deepak's friend. "What is wrong with you?" She pushed him to the sofa. Deepak ran to her before I did.

"What happened?"

"He kissed me!"

"Look it was nothing—"

Deepak leaped forward and attacked his friend. "What the fuck man!" He barked, punching him on the nose.

"What is your problem? You don't like her anyway."

Deepak punched him again. "How dare you—she's my girlfriend!" They wrestled on the sofa and fell off of it. They hit themselves to the tea table, tried to stand up, but pulled each other back on the floor and rolled about fighting.

"Stop," Alisha was slowly recovering. "Let it go—"

"What is going on?" Radhika had come out of the bathroom.

Minutes later the boys let go of each other. They had bleeding noses, bruised cheeks, and fists, and could hardly stand up straight.

"Look, man, hear me out…"

"Leave," screamed Deepak. "Get out."

The friend raised his arms in surrender. "Okay…" He took his bag and swayed out of the door.

"Dee," Alisha ran to his side. "Are you okay?"

"Should I get some ice?" asked Radhika.

"I'm fine," said Deepak in a slurry voice. He slumped on the sofa and winced as Alisha applied some ice on his cheeks. Then, he passed out on the sofa.

"I'll ask everyone to leave," said Radhika.

"No, it's fine," protested Alisha. She went to get a blanket from her room to put it on Deepak.

However, Radhika called everyone upstairs and made them leave. She asked the girls to call her after they reached home. One of Deepak's friends offered to accompany them in the cab. Radhika slept in her room and I slept in Alisha's.

When we awoke the next morning, Alisha complained of a migraine headache. Strangely, I didn't have a hangover. I felt fresh. We noticed the sofa was empty as soon as we got out of the room.

"Dee left?" asked Alisha, with a tinge of disappointment in her voice as she walked past the sofa.

"Yes," said Radhika, rolling her eyes. Radhika was dressed for work, which meant both of us could get the bathroom for ten minutes each before running out of time.

Alisha went to the kitchen to make herself some coffee. Radhika poured milk into her cereal bowl and sat down to eat.

"He made such a fuss in the morning."

I was brushing my teeth and heard snippets of their conversation.

"He was complaining he didn't have clothes for work. What am I supposed to do? I'm sorry but my boyfriend doesn't like anyone else wearing his clothes," Radhika was saying in an agitated tone.

"No—I understand."

"...Sore muscles and a headache... I gave him an Aspirin... He was looking like shit Ali," said Radhika. "His face was still marked. So, I told him to call in sick. But, he yelled at me."

"He had the 'All-Hands Meeting' today..." said Alisha. "I'm so sorry he bothered you."

I came out, and Alisha went to the washroom. I smiled at Radhika and sat down on the sofa opposite her.

"There's some cereal if you like," she pointed to the carton on the kitchen island. I poured myself some and sat down to eat. We chatted a little and she left for her office, which was right around the corner from the apartment complex. How lucky!

By the time Alisha came out, we were running late. Immediately, she booked a cab on an app on her cellphone. "The cab is five minutes away, let's go."

"Why can't they provide a cab?" complained Alisha as the silver hatchback taxi wriggled through the peak hour traffic and reached the gates of Ecospace.

"You faced it too?" I asked. I told her how Kavana had raised her eyes and flatly refused when I had asked her if I could avail the cab facility in office.

"Just because we're juniors—come on. There's no rulebook that states the lowest level employees can not avail cab facilities."

"And, they have policies that say all employees will be treated equally regardless of their position. What a load of bullshit!" I said, as we paid the fare and got out of the cab.

We went upstairs to our separate floors, and I sneaked into my seat as quietly as possible. Of course, I couldn't escape the sarcastic smirk and raised eyebrows of Chetan that told me he knew what I was up to. I sighed and rolled my eyes at him as

I switched on my system. Bhoomija looked at me in disapproval as well. I wanted to bark at her to act like a normal friend, but then she would never get it. So I let it go. A few minutes later, she pulled me to the break out area. As I got up, my gaze automatically went to a seat two rows ahead. Both of us had developed this habit of checking for Kavana each time we got up so she wouldn't catch us in any leisurely condition. Unfortunately, Kavana was on her seat, resting against a pathetic pale pink pillow that she brought from her house. Her head was bent over her cellphone and she was scrolling. Sometimes, I felt like blowing her tiny head off with my fist.

"We'll come back quickly," said Bhoomija, following my gaze. To avoid the barrage of messages from Kavana asking us where we were and why weren't we on our desk, like she did on a previous occasion when we took a five-minute break to go to the washroom, we decided to not lock our systems. This way our Lync messenger statuses would show as 'Available' even when we were not physically present at our desk.

Chetan gaped at me, and then at my system and back at me as were leaving. I quickly ran back. I'd rather be reprimanded for a five-minute absence than have Chetan fool around on my system.

"Come, will you?" Bhoomija grunted in exasperation as I locked my system.

The cool air in the break out area was a blessing for once. I forgot all about Kavana and Chetan and instantly felt like I was on a holiday, though the view outside the window was a dried-up lake and barren land.

"So, tell me. What's up?" I asked, adjusting my butt on the tiny seat of the bar stool in a manner that I didn't fall off. I wondered if I had put on weight as Nishant had pointed out the other day.

Bhoomija was filling a glass with hot water. She had picked up this new habit of drinking green tea to lose weight from her roommates. She dipped the tea bag into the glass as she sat down beside me. She offered me some from her cup.

I choked on the first sip and handed the glass back to her. "Are you trying to kill me?"

She laughed.

"Honestly, poison shouldn't be the antidote for fat," I said, my tongue still hanging out, and a guttural sound coming out of my mouth as if my stomach was cringing from within.

She chuckled and easily took a swig of it. "No pain, no gain."

"Touché," I said, mockingly. Bhoomija said the most clichéd dialogues at times and brimmed as if she had come up with them all by herself.

"But for you, there's an easier way," she went on. "I saw this poster on the canteen wall this morning. Our office is hosting Yoga classes on Mondays. You want to go?"

"Sure."

She made a gagging sound as she gulped the last of the green tea and put the glass in the basin.

"Do you drink?" she asked me out of the blue.

How did she know about yesterday?

I slowly weighed my answer.

"Occasionally. Why?" I was certain she would judge me.

"My roommate bought a bottle of vodka from the wine shop yesterday," she said, excitedly. "And I had a shot."

"OH!" I beamed raising my eyebrows. "Did you like it?"

"Yes. I mixed it with Sprite. It was good," she went on. "We are planning to drink properly tonight. More than one shot."

"Aha?" I winked at her. I told her a few drinking games to play—Boardgames, Never Have I Ever, Truth or Dare. "There's a game you can play while watching TV—I don't know what it's called—every time a certain celebrity says a certain catchphrase, you take a shot. That's the fastest way to get everybody drunk."

I was pleasantly surprised she was on board with the drinking culture. It meant I could share more secrets with her. I told her about the house party with Alisha but refrained from telling her anything about Deepak or the incident that happened.

Bhoomija, on the other hand, told me she and Tarun had been texting each other back and forth since their first date. I teased her until her cheeks turned pink. To be honest, I didn't think Tarun and Bhoomija would hit it. But, it seemed I was wrong. He enjoyed her company as much as she did his. Perhaps, they were going to be a couple after all.

The time for a decent break had passed, and we had to force ourselves to go back to our seats. As expected, Kavana didn't disappoint. The moment I unlocked my system, I was barraged by a ton of messages.

Eight

Alisha was flighty throughout lunch. When I met her for coffee later, she was constantly checking her phone. I asked her if everything was all right and she nodded. As if on cue, her phone lit up with Deepak's call. She jumped up and picked it. She told me she would be back in a minute and went out of the canteen. Ten minutes later she was back. By then the waiter brought her coffee to our table. I was munching on some cookies. I had given up pretending to like coffee, even if that made me less of an adult in others' eyes.

I raised my eyebrows at her.

"Actually," said Alisha, weighing her words. "Dee's friend apologized."

"Oh," I said. I was still angry about the way he had treated her last night and I was sure she was too, so I let her continue.

"I accepted the apology."

I gaped at her.

"Nobody goes around kissing their best friend's girlfriend and then says they are sorry!" I said. I was so appalled I couldn't contain myself. "What does Deepak have to say about it?"

"Look, I know he's an asshole. But, I don't want to make a big deal out of it. Besides, Dee forgave him too."

I couldn't believe she had forgiven him.

"There's no point in dragging this incident. Forget it ever happened, okay?"

I didn't want to agitate her further, so I dropped the topic. I had heard that people's response to danger or trauma was fight or flight. It seemed to me like Alisha not only chose flight physically but also mentally she wanted to run away from it. As long as it restored her peace, I did not say anything.

"Be careful," I added. I felt protective of her for some reason. In a short period, we had become such close friends. "Don't trust people like him."

Her lips curled into a warm smile and she nodded, pouring an entire packet of brown sugar into her coffee, unlike her habit.

Bhoomija and Tarun were drinking coffee at a table opposite us. Lately, they had been spending a lot of time together, despite Kavana's warning. Lunch, coffee, afternoon walks—I ran into them all the time. Bhoomija was narrating something to him animatedly when she caught me looking at her. I smiled and she waved at me. Later, she told me she was telling Tarun about a Korean TV show she followed when we were back in the project bay. The English TV serials on her laptop were now replaced by Korean shows. And, she constantly hounded me to watch them. I felt it was too much effort to watch a show with subtitles, but she did not mind going that extra mile one bit for her 'K Dramas.' Chetan eavesdropped like he occasionally did whenever we chattered excitedly and offered his expert opinion on something completely off-topic. This time it was about the batting average of a sportsman. We readily agreed, afraid that he would go into details, and the time on our systems read seven-thirty already. We bade him good-bye, and left through the central archway, avoiding Kavana and the deadly stares she gave us whenever she saw us leaving for home.

"Happy drinking!" I yelled as Bhoomija and I parted ways at the entrance.

*

We hadn't been given any significant work, though we had by then learnt most of the module from Tarun. Also, he wasn't going to go away from the project any time soon. There were rumours that the senior manager had bashed Kavana instead, for her mastermind plan of replacing Tarun overnight. Her mousy face had grown more hostile over the days. She constantly sent emails to us whenever we went to lunch, coffee, or the loo demanding explanations as to why we weren't on our desks. Bhoomija and I could no longer safely go to the break out area.

Bhoomija caught me as soon as I came to the office that morning and thrust her phone in my hand.

"Guess what," she said excitedly. "I had gone to *Central Mall* yesterday. Look what I tried."

It was a picture of her in the dressing room of the mall. She was wearing a silk red gown that hugged her body in all the right places and made her appear ten kilograms thinner. It had a crystal in the centre that set it apart and gave it a regal look.

"You look sensational," I said, swiping to see if she had clicked more pictures.

"Thanks," she said, blushing shyly. "But, I didn't buy it."

"Why not?" I asked her. I remembered her telling me that she had always wanted to wear gowns and frocks like Sonam Kapoor. I partly knew the answer: her parents wouldn't approve of it.

"Well, firstly, my parents would kill me," she said. I knew it. "And secondly, it costs three thousand rupees."

"Ah," I sighed. Even if she did buy it, she would have to hide it from them at all times she said.

"Three thousand rupees for a dress. It's not made of gold!" she exclaimed. That was half the rent she was paying for her stay in Bangalore, and adding her food and other domestic expenses it would mean zero savings for that month. She told me it was not worth it, but I could see how badly she wanted it. She had never seen herself in a dress like that. And she loved it.

My computer buzzed with a ping.

ALISHA: Hey, where are you? I've some news for you!

ME: Hi, tell me?

ALISHA: Canteen. Meet me in five.

I craned my neck to see past the barrier on my desk. Kavana was on her seat.

ME: I can't. The devil is in her seat.

ALISHA: I promise it won't take more than two minutes.

I took another look at Kavana. She was bent over her cellphone as usual. But, her laptop was opened to her inbox page, showcasing her as a diligent employee who was not in the least bit interested in the matching lottery game that she was playing on her phone. Curiosity got the better of me and I pinged Alisha.

ME: I'll be there in two.

I locked my desktop and sneaked out through the rear entrance, taking the roundabout route, and came to the elevators. When I went downstairs and was disappointed to not find her. To my relief, the elevator doors opened a moment later and I saw Alisha.

She was wearing a green silk top and tights. As she strode towards me, the wind swept her soft caramel hair and made it fly, ever so slightly. She looked radiant, reflecting the summer sun even when she didn't try.

"Hi," she said, beaming.

I gave her a suspicious smile. "Hi."

She took me to the café and our two-minutes' break turned into ten. "Cookies on me."

"So?" I said, sitting in the empty corporate bistro. "What's up?"

"Dee and I are moving in!" she said. I was stupefied.

"What?" I asked sincerely hoping I heard her wrong.

"We're going to live together."

I gave her another chance, but she didn't change her answer.

"Oh," I blurted, urging myself to say something nice, and not what I truly thought of that, as she was so elated. "N—Nice."

"You remember Radhika?" she asked. I nodded. I had met her two days back—unless I suffered from short-term memory loss, which I didn't—it was obvious I would remember her. But, I let her continue. "She is going to Jaipur for work… For a couple of months. When I told Dee about it, he suggested we should live together. He will move in."

"He suggested?" I asked, nodding and grinning with her. "Great."

"Isn't it?" she went on. "I mean I know what you're thinking. My landlord doesn't stay here, and even if he did, he didn't specifically mention that I couldn't live with a guy—and the others in the apartment don't mind—so it shouldn't be a problem."

"Fantastic!"

She had told me how unsupportive her friends had been about their relationship and how she could never speak about her boyfriend with them. I didn't want to make her feel unwelcome to share, so I tried to look as upbeat about her latest decision as she was. But, in a corner of my mind that was a bit foggy and unclear, I feared she was doing a terrible mistake. Speaking of terrible mistakes, I spotted Chetan at the canteen entrance. The worst, however, was him spotting us.

"Aleeesha!" he said, showing his teeth. "Mademoiselle…"

Alisha gave him an uncomfortable smile.

"What brings you here early in the morning? au Bon Pain café… Cookies, eh? Let me get myself a coffee…"

He plunked a chair between us and went to the counter. We scowled at each other behind him, but we knew we couldn't get up and leave. I was going to be delayed further.

He continued to act cocky and flirty with her as I expected and I munched on my cookies and constantly checked my phone for the time.

"So, how's the writing coming along?" he said, suddenly, making me lift my head from my cellphone.

"It's—"

"Are you still daydreaming? Or have you written a book yet?" he asked smugly. I bit my tongue, and my jaw tightened. From the corner of my eye, I looked at Alisha and wondered if she was smiling.

"Look, if you truly want to be a writer, why don't you join a college or something? Join a university in Delhi or Mumbai. Get a degree in literature. Do you smoke?"

"Excuse me?" I wished he would shut up.

"Of course you don't. You should sit with a couple of creative people—have a smoke—discuss politics, religion, football—have you ever taken drugs?"

"No."

"Do you think you'd become a writer by writing in the comfort of your bedroom? Who's even going to read your story? You should go out there—I'm telling you—get out of here first. The world is full of struggling artists and writers—you should try some dope with them—stimulants—see colours—discuss varied stuff."

How would any of that make me a writer? I wanted to tell him to stuff his suggestions up his behind and shut up.

"It's getting late," I said. My head was aching viciously.

"Yes, I have a ton of work. I have to leave too," Alisha took my cue and got up.

"Yes… yes. Go ahead," said Chetan "Think about what I said..."

When I went back upstairs, who should I find at my desk, but Kavana. My luck was eternally screwed. I lied that I had gone to the lavatory seeing her displeased expression, but she continued to look at me like I was filth. She made us open the office Time Tracker website. It was to track your activity for every hour that you spend in the office. After months of being in the project, she had finally given us access to it. However, she made us mark most of our hours as 'Idle.' Upon our protest that we had worked on a few issues, attended KT sessions, among other things, she said curtly that they didn't matter and marking 'Idle' wouldn't be a problem for us since we were new. We did as we were told as there was little left to argue.

The moment she left, Bhoomija pounced on me enthusiastically. Tarun had invited her to a rooftop restaurant in the central area of the city over the weekend. Bhoomija had a hunch that he was going to propose her since he told her he had something important to tell her and it was crucial that she didn't take a rain check. She canceled her bus tickets at once and told her parents she was working on the weekend so she wouldn't be able to make it to the village. What a smooth liar she had become. I teased her and she winked. For the rest of the day she pestered me to choose an outfit for her date. She asked me if she should say *yes* as soon as he asked—would it seem too desperate—should she make him wait for a day and then say yes?

It was a day of relationships. Both my close friends were making progress in their love lives and I was happy for them. As for my own—I picked up my phone and called Raghav on the way home.

Nine

The next week my mind pondered over the rubbish that Chetan had stuffed into it. Did I need a college degree to become a writer?

I searched on Google for the top ten arts and literature universities in India and found a few. The idea of pursuing a bachelor's degree all over again didn't appeal to me. I looked for a Master of Arts in them, and if they accepted B.E graduates. Most of them required a Bachelor of Arts degree for applying. And convincing my parents would be a Herculean task. They hadn't been too keen on my writing during my school days either; they only cherished my academic scores. The year I had written a story, had I not scored the first rank in school, I know the lecture I would have to listen to all summer long, like a tape on repeat mode. So, I wasn't going to tell them yet, particularly when they had dropped hints about taking me on a trip to Switzerland.

I felt someone lean on my chair. I jumped and closed all the tabs on the browser.

"You?" I yelped, breathing a sigh of relief. "I thought it was Kavana."

Bhoomija gave a halfhearted laugh. "Were you searching for a college?"

With sunken eyes and messy hair, she looked weather-beaten. She had donned an old pair of *salwar kameez* that hung loosely on her shoulders.

"Forget that," I said, turning my full attention to her. "How was your date? Did you say yes? Are you guys *'officially'* dating now?" I asked laughing at my lame pun.

At this, her face turned pale. "NO!" she warned, putting a finger to her mouth. "We are not."

She quickly grabbed a chair and sat next to me. She looked from her left to right to make sure nobody overheard, and then narrated the whole incident to me.

On Friday evening, Bhoomija had gone to her paying guesthouse after office and had turned her entire wardrobe inside out. She had thrown a dozen pairs of salwar kameez on the bed and found nothing she liked. Therefore, she had skipped dinner and sneaked out to *Central Mall.* She had bought the red gown with the crystal at the centre. The next morning, she had gone to the parlour to get herself waxed, and set her hair into curls and spent whatever was left of her salary that month. By evening, she was ready for her date in the silk gown, silver earrings, a small purse and a pair of stilettoes that she had borrowed from her roommate. She showed me the *selfie* she had clicked on her cellphone before leaving her room.

"Scintillating," I remarked.

She had then caught an auto-rickshaw to the restaurant. It was a breezy evening, she told me, and her arms felt cold. She had reached the venue on time, paid the auto-driver and had taken the elevator to the roof.

The diner had been made of tiles that looked exactly like wood to those who didn't look closely. Furnished with metal chairs and round tables, the larger ones in the centre and the couples' tables along the balcony, it looked like a sit-out in a terrace garden. Bougainvillea and money plant creepers hung on the balcony railings; there were purple and white orchids and a few other show plants. A soft orange hue from the lampposts lit the place. Bhoomija had spotted Tarun with little difficulty. He was effortlessly attractive in a black T-shirt and a clean shave she had observed.

"Wow…"

He had chuckled softly when he saw her. Bhoomija had blushed and settled in the chair opposite him. They had made small talk of which Bhoomija remembered nothing, as she had been preoccupied with the thoughts of him telling her that he loved her. A waiter had stopped by their table, and Tarun had asked him to come back later. Bhoomija stopped fidgeting and sat raptly.

"Tell me about your dreams?" he had said.

She knew what she wanted to say, but had bit her lip to keep her mouth shut.

"You must have *some* dreams?" he had prodded on. "What are your goals in life?"

"I haven't thought about it," she had answered frankly.

"Let me rephrase that," he had sighed and leaned forward. "Where do you see yourself in the next five years?"

"I—I see myself progressing—manager at Global Software."

The waiter had come back to their table. Tarun had let out another sigh. He had scanned the menu and closed it while Bhoomija still looked at hers.

"Two chocolate milkshakes," he had said.

"Right. Anything else I can get for you sir?" asked the waiter. "Madam?"

Tarun had rolled his eyes. "Do you want any cookies?"

Bhoomija had shaken her head.

"That'll be all," he had said to the waiter and handed him the menu cards.

"So, where were we?"

"We were talking about our dreams," Bhoomija had reminded him with an allusive smile. "What's your dream by the way?"

"I dream of becoming a millionaire in the next five years. In fact in the next two years."

"Wow!"

"But, that's enough about me. Let's talk about you? What do you dream of owning in the next five years? If you were given a crore—"

Tarun's phone had begun to ring. He had seen the name, opened a tiny notebook and pen from his pant pocket and given it to Bhoomija.

"Tell you what—think about the three things you would buy if you had a crore—and write it down here. I've got to take this—"

At this point, Bhoomija told me she had felt fortunate to have a boyfriend who cared so much about her dreams. When he came back, she had written her three things, and had finished half of her chocolate drink.

"Sorry. It was my boss. I couldn't say no," he had taken the note from her.

"Kavana?"

"Not that boss. Remember I told you about my business? The meeting I had had to cancel when we went for Captain America?"

"Yes," Bhoomija had recollected at once.

"No more secrets. I'm going to let you in on something today," he had said, clapping his hands together. "Listen carefully, 'cause we can make your dreams come true."

"I'll be a manager at Global Software in five years?"

"Tell me honestly," he had scoffed. "Do you think Kavana will readily promote you in every cycle so you can become the manager?"

"I'm not demotivating you. I'm the last person to discourage anyone," he had continued. "I can't predict if you'll become a manager or not. Heck! Even managers at Global aren't well paid—F.Y.I. But, I can promise you that you can become rich enough to buy a villa with a swimming pool, a trip to Dubai, and a Lamborghini in five years."

They were the three things Bhoomija had written on her sheet.

"You haven't heard the best part yet," he went on. "You can earn it from the comfort of your home, living the life that you're currently living."

And that's when her instinct had kicked in. It was too good to be true.

"I know what you're thinking. It *is* possible. Trust me. All you have to do is make one decision."

Suddenly, Bhoomija's curiosity was piqued. How could one decision of hers change everything?

"But that can wait," he had said. "First, I want to give you something. The reason why I called you here—"

Bhoomija had braced herself as he bent down to pick something from a bag near his leg. Her heart had hammered in her throat.

"It's one of the finest—something really special—you're *gonna* love it."

Would he go down on his knee? She had wondered. There were a lot of people around, and she had looked to make sure nobody was watching them. She had covered her mouth with her hands, in anticipation, as he had come up and placed it on the table.

An orange bottle.

"He gave you an *orange* bottle?" I asked her incredulously, and both of us burst out laughing. "Well, that's the first time I heard that… No wonder you said no."

"Not just *any* orange bottle," she went on. "It was a bottle of *Doctor Grime's Belly Burner Shake!"*

I covered my mouth to stop myself from bursting out again.

"Premium. Limited stock. And it cost me four thousand rupees. For a freaking shake! That was the extra money my parents had given me to use in case of an emergency," said Bhoomija. "I can't believe he talked me into buying it."

"So, he never proposed to you?"

Bhoomija shook her head.

"I was so foolish," she said, sulking in her seat. "He called me fat. He asked me if my new year's resolution was to lose 10kg? I was so stupid to think he was in love with me."

"What a douche!" I said, sympathizing with her. "So, all he wanted was for you to buy his weight loss shake?"

"That's not all," she said. "He wants me to be a part of it. Invest in his business. He said the market was abundant and showed me pictures of the luxury hotels where he and his partners partied every Friday. He said he has some international partners and they are planning to hold their next success party in Dubai or Malaysia. Apparently, there are only two slots left and the reason he is offering it to me is that he sees potential in me and cares about my future!"

"Don't go for it Bhoomi," I said. "It's a scam."

"He wanted me to invest 14 lakhs in it. I refused, straightaway. Then, he said he had quoted a high price so I could reap the maximum benefit, but even 4 to 5 lakhs would be a good start. When I told him I didn't have that kind of money, he asked me to take a loan," she went on. "—Without telling my parents. He said not only will I have the money back within a year but also it'll be double."

"Did you?"

"I'm not as dumb as I look!" she said.

I bit my lip.

"I wanted to go home. And he wouldn't let me. He kept telling me the figures he was making in that company. I can see why he's succeeding. He harassed me into buying that shake!"

"This network marketing is catching on these days—"

"He asked me not to tell anyone in the office about it. Kavana was right about him," she said, angrily. "He's so cunning."

"I hope you're not talking about me."

We jumped at the sound. It was Chetan, eavesdropping as usual.

"No Chetan, not every cunning person is you!"

Bhoomija was getting into a better mood. Chetan laughed and took his seat.

"Hey," said Tarun, taking his system opposite ours. "Did you think about it?"

Bhoomija gave him a pasted smile and nodded. She spent the rest of the day avoiding him. She joined Alisha and me for lunch in the canteen and was irritable for the most part. Alisha was in the opposite mood. Deepak had moved his stuff to her apartment, and they had gone shopping over the weekend.

"How's Raghav?" she asked. I had been hoping she wouldn't. "What's going on with you guys? You never tell."

"All good," I said, quickly. Raghav and I had fought over the weekend. I felt it too silly and personal to share it even with Alisha.

"Who is Raghav?" asked Bhoomija.

Alisha mouthed the word 'sorry' from across the table.

"A friend," I said.

"Alisha," I said swiftly cutting Bhoomija's interrogation. "Do you want to join us for Yoga classes today?"

Bhoomija took the bait and forgot about Raghav. Alisha refused. Bhoomija forced me to eat fast and skip the afternoon walk so that we could go upstairs, log in and come back down in time for the class.

It went as planned. We took the central archway to get out of the project bay at exactly 4 'o clock and missed Kavana by a millisecond, who was on her way to the washroom. I had brought a change of clothes and I hid that cover behind me as we got into the elevators. We went straight to the women's lavatory on the ground floor. In a building full of formally dressed people, it would be a cakewalk to spot me. I crossed my fingers as I made my way from the washroom to the Yoga class in my bright pink workout gear. Bhoomija didn't want to change and in a minute I saw why: a couple of people ogled at me like I was wearing a swimsuit in office.

We kept our phones and my bag to one side and picked up a green foam mat from the shelf. We were in the middle of an *asana* when a loud ring echoed in the room.

"It's yours," Bhoomija nudged me.

I cursed and opened my eyes. I ran to the shelf. It was a call from an unknown number; I picked it up uncertainly and excused myself out of the room.

"Is it Kavana?" panted Bhoomija, following me.

I shook my head and spoke into the phone, "I'm sorry, you must have me confused for someone else—yes—yes—Sanchita—but I didn't order anything…I'll be there."

"Where are we going?"

"There's some package for me. Where do they get delivered here?" I asked pulling Bhoomija along with me to the back entrance. After a couple of seconds, we spotted the delivery boy and he walked to us.

"Sanchita?" he asked, handing me a cardboard box.

"Yes."

"Here's the package for you from Morning-Glory-dot-com."

"But, I didn't order anything," I said, trying to give back the package.

"Sorry, no refunds or replacements."

I looked at Bhoomija for help. She was as confused as I was. Who would send me something to my office address? "Is there a name? Who paid for it?" I asked, opening the package. It was a bunch of six fine roses. Red, long-stemmed, held together by a thin rope and a card that said 'Have a Wonderful Day.' I couldn't help but smile.

"How charming!" exclaimed Bhoomija, peering into the box.

"No name madam—but there's a number."

Instantly I realized who it was. At the same time, a familiar phone number stared at me.

"Can you sign here please?"

"Give me a minute," I said, all the excitement from earlier dying. His phone was not reachable.

"Look, I don't want this. Please take it back and refund the buyer—"

"Ma'am it can not be taken back. It's delivered fresh daily. No returns—" he argued. "If you will please sign here… I have a long day. Six more packages to deliver."

I reluctantly signed and took the bunch.

"Raghav!" I said to the questioning look on Bhoomija's face.

"Aha! I knew it," she said, grinning triumphantly. "Just a friend?"

My phone rang, and I jumped. "Hello."

"Yes, I got them," I said, grimly. "What was the need for it? No—honestly, I didn't want it. You can't just send me gifts and patch up—that's not what I want—you do know why we fought right—so communicate—this is not over—fine."

I looked at Bhoomija who was watching me, and I gave a pasted smile. It made me so angry that Raghav was making me look bad in front of my friends.

"Yes—they're lovely. Thank you so much," I said, and ended the call.

When we finished yoga, I went to the lavatory to change.

"I can't go back to the project with this," I said, trying to stuff the roses into my bag, but it was too small for the bunch. "Didn't you see the way people looked at me? Thank god we don't know anyone in yoga."

"Don't discard it," said Bhoomija, taking offense as if she had gifted it.

"I'm not," I said. I had an idea. I pulled her to the elevators and clicked on the seventh-floor button.

It was the first time I went to Alisha's project bay. Dubious, I called her standing at the door.

"Come in," said Alisha.

"Can I leave these with you?" I asked her handing over the bunch of roses.

"Let me guess. Loverboy?"

I bit my lips and nodded.

"Everyone in my project will know I have a boyfriend if I walk-in with this. And Kavana hates me enough—"

"Don't worry, I'll keep it for you," she said. "Nobody in my project cares."

I thanked her and we left.

"I tell you everything," said Bhoomija, indignantly as soon as we got into the elevators. I knew this was coming. I told her about Raghav and me after that. Well… almost everything.

We walked in through the central entrance as inconspicuously as we could, sat down on our seats as if we had never left and unlocked our systems. Instantly, I turned to Bhoomija. She looked as stunned and scared as I was. As I re-read the email, a message popped on my Lync messenger.

ALISHA: Why can't my boyfriend ever send me flowers?

Kavana marched to us from her desk. I minimized Alisha's message without replying.

ALISHA: Dee and flowers? Who am I kidding?

ALISHA: He's such a doofus!

"Where have you two been?" barked Kavana. I minimized the Lync message but not before Kavana saw it. I prayed for Alisha not to message again. "You went to the gym, didn't you?"

"No—"

"Don't lie to me. I saw you in that pink dress!" she looked livid and I thought it best not to correct her. "You come here to work or go to the gym? There's been a major incident. The client needs immediate analysis."

"Send a response email right now," she told Bhoomija. "Keep me and the team in the loop."

"And you," she said turning to me. "Send me an email explaining why you weren't available on your desk for hours."

"But—"

"Right now," she yelled as she left. "Don't forget to mark idle on your timesheet."

I cursed her under my breath and Chetan laughed.

"Of all the days, we had to get major work today?" asked Bhoomija, with a shrug.

"I have a feeling she did it on purpose."

"At last, she gave us some work," said Bhoomija.

I nodded and we began to work on it together. The incident took a week to resolve as Bhoomija strictly forbade us from taking Tarun's help.

Ten

I opened my iPhone and was reading an eBook, a classic tale of the Civil War when Alisha joined me at the reception lounge downstairs. Since I couldn't carry paperbacks, this was the easiest way of doing it without any misgivings. It would've been hell to stay here for ten hours every day if not for the eBooks.

"Give me a minute," I said reading the last paragraph on the page. Meanwhile, she rang her boyfriend. Alisha wanted to go home early these days as Deepak was living in her apartment.

"Shall we have pizza today?" I asked her when she finished talking to Deepak.

"You want to tell me what happened?" asked Alisha as we walked down the block in the scorching heat of the noon.

The pizzeria was a few blocks down the campus. Whenever one of us was having a bad day we would end up there. Owing to which we both had put on a few kilos. I had to buy a few palazzos for office since I didn't fit into my old pants anymore, and they made my legs look like that of a baby elephant. Alisha grew from extra small to medium size, so it didn't make much of a difference to onlookers, but to her, it was like hitting rock bottom. But, even that was not reason enough to dissuade us from eating.

"Three guesses who pissed me off?"

"Don't need three," said Alisha. "Kavana."

"Yes. And Bhoomija too," I said, looking over my shoulder. I told her about how Kavana had only been giving work to Bhoomija for the past days.

"Today, Kavana assigned three incidents to Bhoomija," I said, panting as we crossed the lane. "And none to me. When I asked her, she plainly refused stating *'no need, Bhoomija will handle it.'* All these days we had been working on it together. Now even Bhoomija is acting all high and mighty."

We had forgotten that it was a Friday, and the pizzeria would be jam-packed. The air inside was hot and smelled of cheese and sweat. We settled into a small table at the corner after waiting in the queue. We treated ourselves to a large double cheese tomato and bell-pepper pizza. The ratio went like this: the sadder we were, the more cheese we would add on top.

"Yummalicious!" I exclaimed taking a bite and forgetting my boss.

"Your team lead is such a bitch man." As Alisha said it, I saw Kavana standing at the pizza counter. She turned back and looked in our direction.

"Shh..." I whispered, hiding my face under the table. "That's her."

"Relax, I don't think she heard us," said Alisha as I came back up. Kavana had come with the manager, Vishal. They took a parcel of pizzas and went upstairs.

"What does she have for breakfast? An entire lipstick?"

I laughed. "Shh..."

"We can't keep saying Kavana or team lead. She'll catch me someday," I said. "Think of a code word."

"Your team lead's like," she fumbled with a mouthful, *"Ursula!"*

"Phoebe Buffay's sister?" I asked, referring to the character from the prominent TV series F.R.I.E.N.D.S. I couldn't see the resemblance.

"No. The *Disney* villain: *Ursula,"* said Alisha.

"God, you're right," I chuckled. "Scheming and double-crossing—she even has two eels trotting by her side."

"Mine is no better," offered Alisha. "Evil bitch dumped a truckload of work on me this week. It's humanly impossible to finish."

"Cruella de Vil," I said and we both agreed.

"Who was that with Ursula?" she asked, "What's with the suit?"

"He's the manager, Vishal," I said. "There must be some client meeting—that's why he's dressed up."

"I'll bet she's having an affair with him," said Alisha, eagerly.

"Oh god, don't start that again," I said, rolling my eyes. "She's not."

"But, mine is," said Alisha, confidently. "I spotted them near the *Xerox* machine."

"So?" I asked, raising my eyebrow.

"That's the only spot where the surveillance camera doesn't span on our floor," said Alisha. "What do you think they doing there alone?"

I laughed. "For all you know, they could be doing something else—like taking a photocopy maybe—have you considered that?"

"They were not," said Alisha, sticking to her side of the argument. "They sort of panicked when they saw me."

When I went back to the project bay after lunch, Bhoomija was working on the incidents that Kavana had assigned to her. I took out my cellphone and began reading an eBook. Five minutes later, she called me.

"Sanchi, can you come here for a minute?"

"I thought you were to work on it alone?" A couple of hours ago she wouldn't even let me see her system.

"I just wanted you to check this email," she said. "I have to send it to the client."

Reluctantly, I dragged my chair to her system. I read the email and then looked at her, suppressing a smile. I don't know what came over me, but I was not prepared to help her anymore. If she couldn't even write emails by herself, she didn't deserve to be here in the first place.

"Read it again," I said.

She read it aloud but didn't change a word. Five minutes later, Kavana came running to her desk.

"Did you even read that email before sending it? *Please get back to me if you have any 'douds,'"* barked Kavana. "What the hell is a *doud?"*

I closed my mouth tight, but my shoulders shook with mirth.

"Yes, Kavana—" stuttered Bhoomija.

"Did you mail the second client as well?"

"Not yet Kavana."

"Open your inbox, I'll tell you what to write," said Kavana, pulling a chair and sitting beside her to dictate. "We would require your inputs for further investigation. No—require is R-E-Q-U-I-R-E... no—that's correct..."

I couldn't believe Kavana would rather spoon-feed her than let me work on it. At least I didn't require any assistance to write an email.

"Kavana," I ventured when she was done with the email. "Shall I work on the third incident?"

"That won't be necessary," she said, scowling at me.

"And you," said Kavana to Bhoomija. "Next time, email me, not the clients. I'll mail it to them."

I later realized this was the most foolish thing I'd done as neither Bhoomija nor I benefitted from it, but Kavana. By emailing the clients on Bhoomija's behalf, Kavana took credits for Bhoomija's work. It proved that she had worked on the incidents and Bhoomija had merely assisted her. Bhoomija was blissfully ignorant of the consequences.

I left early that day, without waiting for Bhoomija. The next couple of days Bhoomija walked around with an invisible crown. She became so close to Kavana, that Kavana would ring her up after she left the office and gossip. She even shared her family problems with Bhoomija and sought her advice on it.

Meanwhile, I was plotting on how to ask Kavana for a leave. An opportunity presented itself when I ran into Kavana in the lavatory one-afternoon post-lunch. It struck me then, that I had never taken a holiday before. When I asked her, she gave me a nasty look and refused.

I met Nishant over the weekend and bitched about *Ursula, a.k.a Kavana.* He told me that his brothers were back from Canada, Holland, and Mumbai. He didn't seem too thrilled about it. He gave me some of the Canadian strawberry wafers that his brother had brought for them.

"I don't know what I'm doing with my life," he said, sipping his beer. "I'll be stuck here forever."

"What do you mean stuck here?" I asked, taking a bite of the *ravioli.* "You can join another office. Your bond must be expiring in a couple of months." I looked outside the window of the elegant Italian restaurant in Indiranagar. The pitter-patter of rain mixed with the music of the in-house live band and created a magical tune.

"I'm talking about Bangalore," he said, serving himself a sumptuous amount. "People are going places. And I'm going to remain here forever. If I had a chance to go back and study properly in college…"

"Are you kidding me? If you had the chance to go back, you would live your college days exactly the way you did before…"

"True," he laughed.

"But, nobody will give me a job in another country, onshore opportunities are nil, and MSc. is out of the question," he went on.

"Why are you in such a hurry to get out?" I asked. "I thought you liked it here."

"I do. But, all our college friends, my brothers, sisters, everybody is in a different place—uploading pictures on Facebook—"

"Nishaaaa!" I admonished, using his college nickname. "Stop comparing your life to everybody else's on Facebook. Why do you care what they are doing?" I said punching him on the shoulder. He gave me an embarrassed smile and changed the topic.

"What have you been reading?" he asked.

"Actually, I've been writing."

I was carefully watching his expression.

He had a look of genuine surprise. "What is it about? Can I read?"

I nodded and gave him my cellphone. "It's not a story. Just a few scenes…"

"Oh, that's hot," he said, reading the first one. I showed him a couple of other scenes. "Not bad… You should join them and make a story."

"That's not how it works," I said, grinning.

"No?"

When I told him about my dream of becoming a writer, he didn't mock me like Chetan. We recognized a song the band was playing and hummed along. Then, we took a few pictures and walked in the rain like the old days. I went home and uploaded our photos on Facebook with the caption, 'because we're not having enough fun in Bangalore unless we're posting.'

*

"There's something on your—" I said pointing to her neck. Alisha swiftly pushed a tuft of her hair on it. "Wait a minute—is that a hickey?"

Alisha bit her lip and promptly blushed.

I made a hooting noise.

"Shh… Cruella might be around. It's not seen clearly, is it? I applied ice on it this morning."

We sat under our acclaimed berry tree on the east side of the Ecospace campus after lunch, watching employees of various offices walking past and covering their noses to escape the sweet-smelling smog of faeces coming from the sewage plant. Nothing had changed.

"I'm so sick of this place man," grunted Alisha. "Why do people even walk there when it stinks so badly?"

"Cause they know it stinks lesser than their bosses," I said with a chuckle. "You know, if there was an award for the most hated employee of the year, I would be sweeping it with ease. And the most hated boss award would definitely go to Ursula. In a way, we are perfect for each other."

"I beg to differ. If there was such an award, Cruella would go out of her way to vouch for me."

"I feel so stuffy here. It's like we're on repeat mode daily," whined Alisha. This was probably the hundredth time she had said it in the last few months. We were both slowly falling into depression. "I've been discussing with Dee. Even he wants to get out of Bangalore. We are planning to do MSc. in the USA."

"Awesome," I said, as we walked back to our office building. We went to the library on the last floor of the building, as Alisha wanted to browse some universities without Cruella peeping into her system.

"But wouldn't it be the same afterward, after MSc.?" I asked Alisha.

"Not at all," she answered. "*A.* They won't treat you like shit like they do here. *B.* You'll be given important things to work on—substantial work—not something that wouldn't matter if you dropped dead tomorrow. *C.* It is the United States! You can keep vacationing from one place to another on weekends, and party like cray. You should come too."

"Convincing," I said, browsing some university websites that offered literature and creative writing courses.

She pointed to an image of a university on her system. "I want to live here in California, by the sea. Rent a car, drive up to the beach with Dee daily. He could teach me how to drive. We could chase ice cream trucks and wear anything we want, without being judged. Heck, we could even kiss on the streets! And in a few years, we could buy a villa that overlooked the waters. I want to start my life there."

"Whoa!" I squealed. "Sounds perfect." Though I never thought much of Deepak, when Alisha put it that way, even Deepak sounded like a decent human being. However, there was a thought itching in the back of my mind. If Alisha was serious about moving to the USA, I would lose my best friend in the office.

When I went back to the project bay Bhoomija was ecstatic. Kavana was going to make her the head.

"She's going to make you the team lead?"

"NO! Dummy. Not the team lead. She's going to make me the head of the CRM team—I'll be in charge of all the activities. Can you believe it?"

I couldn't. On the one hand, I felt insanely jealous, and on the other, I had already shrugged and given up on my future in Popshake. I was not going to lick Kavana's feet to get to the top. I pretended to be excited about Bhoomija's news. And she told me that Kavana had hinted it during one of their gossip calls after office, but now she had confirmed it. The entire week Bhoomija floated on cloud nine. She fluttered through the project bay like a swan with bright smiles and gleaming eyes. Even Tarun couldn't spoil her mood anymore.

*

Alisha started preparing for the GREs. We would go to the office library for an hour daily. I would write, while she browsed for universities, filled applications and looked for accommodation. Bhoomija had not come to work since Monday. Kavana had suddenly taken notice of me. She dumped all of Bhoomija's work on my head, but the way she treated me remained the same. I complained about it to Alisha, as we walked in the "fresh air" outside the office.

"I don't know what Ursula's problem is," I whined. "Bhoomija can take leave for five days. But if I ask for a day's leave, and that too two-to-three weeks in advance, I've to go meet the manager? Double standards!"

"What the hell? You're allowed to vacation for at least twenty days in a year. And, you haven't taken a single day off till now," said Alisha. "Are you afraid to ask your manager?"

"He's not in the country." I retorted. "He's onshore and will be back in a month or two. She wants me to wait until then. I need to go to Switzerland in two weeks."

Alisha urged me to use my sick leaves. "Tell her you're unwell like Bhoomija did. She can't do anything then."

"By the way, Bhoomija isn't ill either. That's a cover-up," I said, kicking a pebble on the path. "Her mother is out of town, so Bhoomija had to stay back in her village and cook for her family."

"She's bunking office for that?"

We turned a corner and came to our building. Nothing in the world could've prepared me for what happened next. I entered the building and stopped dead in my tracks. He was sitting on a lounge chair beside the reception desk. My breath caught in my mouth. Somewhere in the distance, I could hear Alisha's voice asking me what had happened. He had spotted me. He got up and walked to me.

"Hi Sanchita," he said with a grin.

"R—R…Raghav," I stuttered. "What a surprise!"

I despised surprises.

"Well, aren't you?" He gave me a cheesy grin. He was wearing a tag around his neck, not like ours. *A visitor's tag?* I wondered who had vouched for him in the company. I still found it hard to believe that he was right in front of me. "Hi, you must be Alisha. I've heard a lot about you," he said giving her a hand to shake.

"Nice to meet you, Raghav," said Alisha with a warm smile.

"You didn't tell me your boyfriend was coming," she whispered to me. "I guess I should leave you two to catch up."

"You should've called," I said to him after she left. My cheeks hurt from grinning continuously.

"I came from Chennai this morning. Thought I'd swing by," he said, "Besides if I had told you I would've missed this look on your face."

"Huh?" Much as I tried, I couldn't shake off the feeling that I was a bit disappointed to see him. And, that is not what a girl should feel when she sees her boyfriend. Maybe it had something to do with our last meet when he had turned up in front of my college, unannounced, and got down on his knees in front of fifty people. And, I had accepted his proposal out of sheer embarrassment. I was glad none of my friends knew about that meet.

"You look so happy," he said. I wondered if he knew me at all. We shared an ice cream in a bistro outside the office. I didn't want to pique Kavana's curiosity.

Raghav told me that he had shifted to Bangalore for a few months. His office was in Whitefield, a few minutes' drive from mine.

"That's great," I said, biting the ice cream.

"At least now we can meet more often. And you can go to bars for drinks with me. Not with some lame-ass buddy."

I chocked on my ice cream. "Are you talking about Nishant?"

"No—why? Do you meet him often?"

"Oh my god," I whispered. "You're here because you saw us—I uploaded that picture on Facebook. And all this time, I thought you had come here for me."

It struck me then that I had never told him anything about Alisha.

"Don't be ridiculous!" he snapped. "I have come here to be with you."

I nodded. The bistro was crowded. Perhaps, I was overreacting. He had come from Chennai to meet me. He had shifted his workplace so we could be together. But somewhere in the back of my mind, a panic alarm went off.

"Is your team lead still troubling you?" he asked, watching me.

I took it as a chance to dispel the cold air between us.

"When doesn't she?" I said dramatically using my hands. "She's not letting me take a few days off. Can you believe it?"

"Do you know what your problem is?"

"Oh no," I said in sotto voce. I knew that look on his face as he leaned in closer.

"You don't have the guts."

My jaw tightened. "Excuse me?"

"I'll bet, you haven't even asked her."

I wanted to give him a piece of my mind, but he had come all the way from Chennai to meet me. The least I could do was be nice. I gave him an agitated smile, stuffed my mouth with the rest of the ice cream, and hoped he'd take a hint.

"You let people take you for granted. Look, just tell her: like it or not, I'm taking a holiday. Simple."

I took a sharp breath and got up. "It's getting late."

"Let me drop you."

"I'll manage."

"We should do this again," he said, sharply, as if he had sensed my thoughts.

"Absolutely." I had already started walking towards my office.

Eleven

Interlaken was a small town of tourist resorts, to the south of Zurich in Central Switzerland, nestled between Lake Thun and Lake Brienz. I had come to Switzerland with my family for a week.

The funny thing was, for the visa, I was required to get an official letter from my office stating that I was on leave. *Yeah right,* if it were that easy. Kavana was not ready to give me a day's leave, let alone grant me a permission letter to vacation in a European country for seven days! Therefore, I took sick leaves, on my own, without giving two hoots for Kavana's approval, and stated on my visa that I was unemployed. Alisha had remarked that that was not a lie: working in Global Software Services was equivalent to being unemployed. By now we had realized that they only needed us for headcount, and treated us like shit. Alisha had turned rebellious and pointed out, *"Anyone can fall ill and take leaves—it's your basic right as an employee."* The downside of it was that every morning for an entire week I had to re-apply the sick leave.

We had boarded the coveted European rail from Zurich, which offered scenic views of streams, mountains, and waterfalls to Interlaken. It took us two hours to reach the Interlaken OST station, close to our hotel.

Towering mountains and lush green meadows of this picturesque town reminded me of Bollywood movies. When I first landed in Interlaken, it looked to me as if the mountain had been cracked open at the bottom and the road to the village had been made. Walking was an uphill task, literally. Everywhere I went I either ran into a red flag with a white cross, billboards of black and white patched cows, cowbells or *'moo'* signs. I hadn't spotted an actual cow though.

As we had traveled during summer, the weather was warm in this village compared to Zurich, at least during the day. I shuddered at the thought of how cold this place would be in winter. A cool wind blew, and the light smell of fresh grass and cigarettes wafted through the air around us.

River Aare, which flowed through the town, was an interesting blue-green colour that offered a great background for a picture. However, I was careful not to post any photographs on Facebook. Only Alisha knew about my vacation.

As soon as we reached the hotel, I asked for the password to the Wi-Fi connection. I crossed my fingers as I checked my emails. I had given Alisha my password and she had promised to write a sick mail for me every morning if I couldn't connect to my email. But, thankfully I could connect to my mailbox. Alisha had assured me she would notify me immediately if any issue came up at the office. And, I had complete faith in her, unlike in Bhoomija. As I had not received any pressing emails from Alisha, I breathed a sigh of relief and enjoyed the rest of the day.

As soon as I woke up the next morning, I wrote an email to Kavana stating I was still unwell and wouldn't be able to make it to office. I termed it in the politest of words and hit send. This sick leave system of mine worked for three days without hindrance. On the fourth day, when I was relishing a croissant with my favourite chocolate spread, *Nutella* in a patisserie below my hotel, I received an email from Kavana.

The mail read like this: *'Hi Sanchita,'* I noted how she would not call me dear—even in an email. *'I tried contacting you earlier today. However, I was unable to reach you on your cellphone. Hope you are aware of the company policy. Since you have taken three days of sick leave without the manager's approval, you will be required to produce a medical certificate for your illness upon your return. Regards, Kavana.'*

If she tried to contact me…

Another email confirmed my fears.

Babe,

Ursula's been asking about you. Heard from Bhoomija at lunch today. I tried calling you immediately and guess what? The recording played in German! Switched off your phone immediately! Probably it'll still tell in German that your phone is switched off—take out your SIM card before Ursula tries to contact you.

Missing you loads,

XOXO

Alisha

PS: Don't forget my Swiss chocolates.

I borrowed my father's cellphone and dialed my number. She was right. It played a voice tape in German. I was so dead!

"What happened?" asked my parents. I told them it was nothing and smiled. To my parents, a boss's disapproval was equivalent to a teacher's admonishment and not getting a promotion was correspondent to failing an exam. Anger and fear were doing the *Pasodoble* in my heart. It was unfair that I had to hide it. I was allowed to vacation in whatever country I chose to. It was not like I was stealing her money to do it! I finished the rest of my breakfast quietly contemplating how I would convince Kavana that *Germany* was my hometown!

Mount Jungfrau was one of the highest peaks of the Swiss Alps in the Bernese region. It was a two-hour journey from Interlaken. After breakfast, we took the local train to Kleine

Scheidegg, Lauterbrunnen, and from there we boarded the Jungfrau Railway, a cogwheel train up the mountain. It was miraculous how the cogwheel of the train latched onto the track at each step as it moved, helping the train balance. As it diligently climbed up the steep mountain, the temperature dropped lower and lower. I pulled my jacket tight and wrapped my arms around myself. My ears popped as they did in airplanes.

We got off at Jungfraujoch, the highest railway station in Europe, underneath the Jungfraujoch col and took the elevator to the Sphinx observatory at the top. We stepped outside for a stroll in the glaciers. To hell with Kavana and my office, the view was breathtaking! I wanted to stay forever.

The snow glistened under the intense rays of the sun. Cold air brushed against my face and made my hair fly underneath my cap. My boot was damp as I walked on the glacier path between two snow peaks. It felt like a scene straight out of the movies. A snowflake fell on my shoulder out of thin air. I looked up. I caught the flake in my hand to check the pattern but it melted on my finger before I could. My momentary disappointment was brushed away when a second flake fell on my nose, and another in my palm. It was so tiny—it looked like a miniature cobweb. It was the first snowfall I had seen, and I knew I wanted to capture its beauty on paper.

My parents hurried me indoors as dark grey clouds approached. The observatory had an ice palace that housed sculptures of penguins, bears, and eagles made purely of ice. I wondered if the sculptures never melted. At a bar in the observatory, my parents sat down with a cup of steaming coffee while I stood at the glass windows watching the Alps and sipped hot chocolate. Setting the cup down, I opened my Notes app and began to write. Everything was so quiet. The whole world had disappeared around me, and it was only the snow and my writing. Even in the biting cold, I felt the warmth around me. It felt golden, if only for a moment. I had never felt this way while sitting in the company and doing my engineering work. I was experiencing a moment of earnest vulnerability and immense power at the same time. I knew this is what I wanted to do for the rest of my life. I wanted to be a writer.

I picked up some souvenirs—cowbells, key chains, and premium Swiss chocolates for Alisha, Raghav, and Nishant. Bhoomija crossed my mind. But then, if I bought her a gift I would have to tell her about the trip. And I couldn't risk that. We boarded the flight from Zurich the next day and reached Kempegowda International Airport in Bangalore in the early hours of the morning. I wanted to sleep in, but my parents wouldn't hear of it.

"Why do you need a holiday? We're back from Switzerland. And nothing is wrong with you. Don't make a habit of bunking," said my mother. "Look if you don't struggle in your life now you will never come up. You should be enthusiastic about going to the office not behave like you're doing everyone a favour by going there."

"We just came back," I yelled in frustration. "I didn't unpack. I haven't even got the medical certificate—I'll go—"

"Medical certificate?" caught my father sharply. "What do you need that for?"

"Ah! She has lied in her office to come to this holiday," smirked my mother.

I gritted my teeth. "I did not lie!"

I had convinced my parents that Kavana had given me an off but an official permission letter for the visa couldn't be given as that right was vested in the hands of the manager who was out of the country at the moment. And now, my house of lies was falling apart.

"Tell me, does your boss know you went to Switzerland or does she think you're suffering from viral fever?"

"Of course she knows," I retorted immediately, "I said medical\certificate just in case. There's no need for it. I'll get ready and go."

"If I was your boss I would've thrown you out," my father went on. "Look at the time. It is 8 o'clock already. Learn to be punctual—"

If I had a jet lag, I wouldn't know. It was nothing compared to the way my head was now pounding. I reached my office at twelve. I had waited in line at the family doctor's clinic on my way to the office and had easily procured a medical certificate for viral fever. I knew Kavana would be waiting to pounce on me. And I didn't want to give her a chance to point fingers.

"Dude," Bhoomija squealed as soon as she saw me. She seemed genuinely happy to see me. I felt guilty for not bringing her a gift.

"Where were you? Why didn't you come to the office all these days?"

"Hi Bhoomija," I said, putting my bag down. "I was not well. I had viral fever."

"For so many days? You can tell me the truth," she said rather insistently. "I won't tell Kavana."

The way she said it I knew Kavana had put her up to this task. "I told you. I had a fever! Do you also need a medical certificate to believe me? Did Kavana ask you to check that as well?"

"I asked out of concern," she said and went back to her system. She's one to ask—she had taken a week off to stay at home and cook.

Alisha greeted me as soon as I logged into the Lync messenger.

ALISHA: Sanchi! Thank god you're here. I was beginning to think you're not coming today.

ME: Aliiii! I missed you.

ALISHA: Come to the canteen? I have some news.

ME: Is everything okay?

ALISHA: NOW!

Alisha went offline. I hated it when she did that. I dialed her cellphone, but it didn't connect. She was probably in the elevators already. I cursed and got up to leave.

"You're taking a break already?" asked Bhoomija.

"No," I rolled my eyes. It hadn't been ten minutes since I was back and she was driving me nuts. "I'll be back in a minute."

The last time Alisha had pinged me with news she had decided to live-in with Deepak. I wondered what disaster she had brought on herself this time. As I got into the elevator, I suddenly remembered that in my hurry to the office this morning I had forgotten her gifts at home.

I hadn't told Raghav I was back. I was afraid he would show up in front of my office again, and the last thing I needed was for Kavana to gossip about my love life.

I pulled Alisha into a hug as soon as I saw her. In all these days as friends, it was the first time we hugged. An invisible wall that I didn't know existed between us was shattered. Something was amiss. She wasn't hugging me back with the same enthusiasm…

"He cheated on me," she blurted.

"What?" I said, letting go of her. I wondered why I was giving her a chance to change her statement. I had heard her perfectly.

"He cheated on me!" she said, loudly. I didn't know what to say.

As silence hung between us, I noticed her eyes were bloodshot red and puffy. She had not applied her eyeliner. Her face was pale and her lips were chapped. Her hair was uncombed and thinning. It was like she had aged in a week. Two prominent worry lines etched her forehead.

"How did you know?" I stuttered, uncomfortably. I was still in a state of shock. I knew he was pathetic, but I hadn't expected him to cheat. For a second, I wondered if there was a possibility that she was mistaken.

She was looking straight ahead, past me. Her eyes had a distant look in them as though she was in a trance. We were sitting on our usual table in *au Bon Pain café.* We hadn't ordered anything yet. I caught the waiter staring at us. I chose to ignore him and urged her to tell me how she had found out.

"On Friday, there was this event in the cafeteria—" she said, "cultural day—some singing, dancing—it was a lame event. But, everybody from my team was there. But Cruella had stayed upstairs. So I thought this was my chance to get out of the office early. I finished my work and left after lunch. I wanted to start the weekend early—go clubbing with Dee—" she hesitated. "I didn't know that asshole would be partying with someone else on his lap!"

"What the fuck—" I covered my mouth. A mental image of that popped in my head, unbidden and made me want to cringe. I hated her boyfriend, but even more now.

"That bitch had her tongue on his throat—when I—I can't," she was stammering, her eyes full of pain, fury, and grief. "She was even wearing some flimsy lingerie! Can you believe it? I'm his girlfriend and I would never bother to do that for him—I feel sick."

"Wait a minute, he brought her to your apartment?"

"Yes," she answered. "Look at his guts. She didn't even know it was my apartment. And when I caught them, he tried to pretend like he was not at fault. He asked me why I hadn't told him I was coming home early. Was I spying on him? He began attacking me."

"How manipulative is this guy!" I was sitting in rapt attention.

"He is. I saw another side of him that day… and to think we've been together for almost five years."

"He didn't even apologize?"

"Apologize? He blamed me for it. He said I don't give him enough freedom and so he had no other option but to cheat. I'm crowding his space? *Bloody ass!* I gave him the space to live in. His parents were sick of him loitering around late nights and they had thrown him out. That's when he had suggested we should live in. I was such a fool…"

Suddenly, she was caught in a fit of a cough so bad that her eyes began to tear up.

I patted her and looked for some water. "Shall I get you some juice?" She nodded and I went to the counter to place an order. When she had told me about them moving in together she had carefully omitted the part where his parents had kicked him out.

When I came back, she seemed to have pulled herself together. She thanked me for the drink and sipped it. So many questions were running in my head. I was curious to find out who the girl was, but I didn't want to ask.

"I'm so sorry I've been ranting to you since you came," she said, putting her glass down. "How was your trip? Tell me all about it."

She was smiling softly for the first time since I met her. I sensed that she didn't want to talk about the incident anymore and so I dropped it too. I told her about the European village and the Alps. I showed her the photographs I had clicked on my phone. She was smiling as she saw them, but a tear trickled down her cheek.

"Ali, let it go," I said, catching her wrist. I couldn't contain myself anymore I was so angry. "That asshole doesn't deserve you."

"I know," she whispered. Then, she got up to leave. She wasn't even letting me comfort her. I told her I would meet her for lunch in a couple of minutes. She nodded. We stood in silence in the empty elevator and I got off at my floor, waving to her. Unbidden thoughts barged into my mind as I walked back to my desk. I had my initial doubts about

Deepak, but even I had begun to believe he truly loved Alisha. They had been together for so long, then why had he chosen to do that? Was she stupid to date a person like him? NO! Can one predict who would cheat on them before it happened? I wondered where Kavana was as I opened the glass doors to my project and went inside. I hadn't seen her in the morning. Chetan greeted me as soon as I came back.

"Ha, look who's here," he quipped, grinning widely. "And I thought you had become an author—doing book tours on the coasts of Africa."

I flushed. People were watching us. I saw Vishal, our manager, walking past my row. I cleared my throat and said quickly, "No, Chetan. I was unwell."

"Ma belle is unwell," he said clapping his hand loudly. The guy in the desk opposite us, where Tarun used to sit, was finding it hard to keep a straight face. I smiled embarrassedly and rolled my eyes at him in a tell-about-it-manner. I didn't know who he was, and I wondered where Tarun was sitting. I later found out from Bhoomija that Tarun had been sacked from the project. So Kavana had got her way? *Shit.*

I ignored Chetan and checked the schedule for the day on the system.

"What have I been telling you? Quit this place. Go do BA or MA," he said. "Everybody here is suffering. It's a life-sucking machine."

"I'll think about it Chetan," I said, cutting him short. I didn't want him to launch into his philosopher mode again. It was far worse than his criticizing and flirting. But, of course, he didn't stop.

"Why don't you learn journalism, eh? That has a lot of potential. Join a university in Mumbai or Delhi..."

I didn't want to do journalism. I wanted to write stories. But I knew if I said another word to him, I would only be allowing him to drill my ears with more advice. So, I turned to Bhoomija. There were two incidents raised by the client that day. Bhoomija was working on one; I offered to work on the other.

"I think you should ask Kavana first," scoffed Bhoomija.

"But I work on the same team," I retorted. She was being so unreasonable. It was not like I was snatching her work.

"Yes," said Bhoomija. "But, she asked me to work on the incidents."

I let out a frustrated sigh. Then, I spotted something on the office timesheets page.

"Bhoomija," I called out to her again, "why have you filled your timesheet with incidents 852 and 875?"

"It was assigned to me," she said, effortlessly.

"Yes, but I worked on them," I said, gaping at her. "You weren't even here when I resolved those incidents. What the hell? Now I've to mark idle on my timesheets for that period?"

"Kavana asked me to mark it on mine," she said monotonously.

I grunted and pushed the keyboard aside. Like boss, like employee. Kavana was stealing credits for Bhoomija's work and now Bhoomija was doing the same to me. Who could I complain to? Kavana was already on her side. I let Bhoomija deal with the work that day and began reading an eBook on my phone. When it was time for lunch, I pinged Alisha and went downstairs.

Twelve

Alisha was sulking again as I had expected. But, to my utter disbelief, Bhoomija joined us. They had been accompanying each other for lunch in my absence. Alisha said she had lost her appetite, and kept checking her phone. But when I insisted, she agreed to have a plain dosa with us. I wondered why she kept looking into her phone. Deepak wasn't texting her. Perhaps, it was out of sheer habit and nothing else. We ate in silence as neither Alisha could talk about her ex, nor I about my trip in Bhoomija's presence. Alisha gave me an apologetic look. I simply shrugged. If they wanted to spend time with each other who was I to stop them?

The small talk we were making: pass the chutney, the weather is so cold today, did you watch the new Avengers movie, was killing me. I was bursting to talk. The minute Bhoomija left the table, we started talking. Alisha thrust her phone in my hand.

"Tell me she's fat," said Alisha.

I knew at once it was the girl with whom Deepak had cheated on her. Alisha had stalked her on Facebook.

"She is," I replied instantly, though I didn't think that.

"I mean what does he even see in her? She's ugly—fat—she is even taller than him—huge. Look at this picture—she doesn't even know how to wear make-up properly. What a dumbass!"

"How did she meet him?" I asked, out of curiosity. I figured my question wouldn't upset Alisha now that we were speaking about her.

"Office. She's his colleague!" said Alisha. "Apparently, she was recently out of a relationship and looking for a rebound."

"How do you know that?" I asked her, wondering if a person's Facebook profile could reveal that much information about them, or if Alisha was that skilled at stalking somebody.

"She told me today," answered Alisha, "when she called to apologize."

"You spoke to her?" I still found it hard to believe—surreal—like it was happening to someone else and not my best friend.

"Yes and guess what, she didn't even know I was his girlfriend."

I gaped at her in disbelief. "She didn't know it was your apartment… She didn't know he had a girlfriend… What does she even know about him?"

"*Dumbass!* Anyway, it isn't her fault. This asshole hasn't told anyone in his office that he has a girlfriend!" said Alisha. "She said she had picked up my name when we—at my apartment that day. Today when Dee—*Deepak* went to the washroom in the office, she checked for my number on his phone and called me."

The evidence in front of our eyes might provoke our minds to change our relationship with someone, but our hearts take longer to process. Even if we break up with someone, we will always call them by the nicknames we had given them.

"You know, he never let me touch his phone," Alisha complained. "And he's given her his password… I guess now I why he never let me touch it."

Alisha's eyes welled. I had never seen her cry until then. She was always pragmatic and in control of her emotions. She quickly turned away from me and started using her mobile. I wanted to reach out to her, place my hand on her back and tell her it was going to be okay. But, she didn't want me to see her tears, so I choose the easy way out and pretended not to see them. Instead, I said the first stupid thing that came to my mind.

"Is that a new game?"

She looked up from her phone, and said softly, "Yes… It's the rage these days. Dee and I—" She stopped herself and cleared her throat. Her voice was thick with emotion when she spoke, but her words were impassive. "You can solve mysteries, find hidden objects, guess the criminal. Everybody is playing it."

"You know you deserve better than Deepak, don't you?" She looked up and held my sight for a moment. Then, she slowly nodded.

I was shocked to see the time on my phone. We had spent 2 hours downstairs. When I told her it was time to get back, she got up slowly. We took the elevators back to our floors. I hated to see her in this vulnerable state. I wished I could say something more to console her, but I couldn't. I told her I would meet her afterward and left.

I walked fast through the central archway, avoiding any eye contact. If anyone realized I was away from my desk for two hours, I'd be roasted alive. I was at the end of the passage when Kavana stopped me.

"Sanchita," Kavana called out from the far end of the room. She was sitting on her desk and watching me with hawk eyes. I gulped. With no choice left, I slowly dragged my feet to her desk.

"Hi Kavana," I said, sporting a fake smile. But, I doubt that hid the guilt that was written all over my face.

"Hi Sanchita," she said, with a smile bigger and faker than mine. "Do you switch off your phone during lunch?"

I was taken aback by her question.

"No—I don't switch it off. My network doesn't connect in the basement—"

"Why is that only when I want to speak to you your phone doesn't connect? Or is your phone as smart as you in avoiding me?"

I wondered if I should explain my phone situation to her in French. Two rows of employees were watching her admonish me. I looked at some of them in the eye and they went back to their screens. This was as much entertainment they could get on a Monday afternoon.

"Anyway, Vishal wants to have a word with you," she said, "Conference room, 4 P.M. today."

She didn't even ask me about my medical reports. Strange… I wondered if the meeting was for that. I strolled back to my desk uncertainly. I had nothing to fear, the medical reports were intact. She wouldn't be able to pin anything on me.

I had an hour to go and nothing to do. So after logging in to Lync messenger and pretending to work, I opened my iPhone and began reading a classic. Bhoomija kept staring at me with accusing eyes but I ignored her. As the meeting time grew closer, I began to feel nervous. First of all, I was surprised Vishal was back from his onshore trip so early. Secondly, I had never had a one to one meeting with the manager before. Why would he want to meet me now? Was taking a leave for a week such a big crime that I must be reprimanded for it? Somehow I had figured out that if a conference room was involved, it was bad news. But still, I took a deep breath and mustered up the courage to go. I took out the medical report from my bag, and I put it in my pocket. It was fake, but there was no way they could prove it. On the way to the conference room, I took out the report again and scanned it. Was my name written on it correctly?

I peeped through the glass walls of two conference rooms and couldn't find them. I was suddenly feeling like peeing. I checked my phone—it was four. Kavana would ring me up in the toilet and still expect me to pick it if I didn't reach the meeting room on time. I would hold myself until the meeting was over. I had peed a while ago. It was the nerves. I could see Vishal's silhouette through the translucent glass of the last room. There was someone next to him, and it was not Kavana.

I pushed the door and put my face inside.

"May I come in?" I asked.

Vishal answered with a polite grin, "come in Sanchita." I recognized the person sitting next to him. The senior manager. Beside them was another man in a suit. I didn't know him. "Take a seat."

I was glad to see a familiar face—Kavana. I tried to smile at her as I sat down. At least she was someone I had interacted with regularly before this meeting, and deep down I felt she would protect me.

"Shall we begin?" Vishal asked Kavana. She simply shrugged. The air in the conference room was getting cooler. My teeth were chattering. I still had the report in my hand. I put it on my lap and decided to show it when they asked.

"Sanchita," said Vishal. I looked up immediately. "You know why you're here, right?"

"Yes—umm—no" I looked from him to Kavana. I wished this ordeal was over and I was back on my system, under that goddamn tubelight.

"We are here to discuss your work in *Popshake,*" said Vishal. "Are you aware that there are certain tasks expected of you, and that as a fresher, your actions are continuously being monitored?"

I nodded. I was still wondering when to give him the medical report that I had come prepared with.

"However, we have come to hear of certain issues with your performance..."

The senior manager pitched in, drowning Vishal's voice. "Tell me Sanchita," he said clapping his hands. "How many hours did you mark as *'idle'* on your timesheet today?"

"F—Five," I stuttered.

"Five in one day? What about last month?" he asked. My throat was drying. "Why is it that you aren't up to the mark when all your peers are doing so well?"

I gulped. "I—" I looked at Kavana. Her chapped scarlet lips were brimming in delight. She was thoroughly enjoying the show. "She hasn't worked on any incident in two weeks."

"Tell me Sanchita," the senior manager was getting impatient and I had lost my voice. Whatever hopes I had of Kavana saving my ass, died. I felt betrayed.

"I completed the tasks you had assigned," I said looking at Kavana.

"You don't take the initiative. That is the problem," she squeaked at me in her shrill high-pitched voice, and then turned to the senior manager, "She doesn't show any interest, Chandran! What do I do?"

"I wasn't assigned any incidents this week."

"She can't handle incidents on her own, Chandran. She cannot work independently. That's why I'm afraid to assign—"

"That's not true—" I had found my voice at last. What a liar! "I have solved incidents independently."

Kavana dismissed it and went on. "Ask her what time she comes to the office every day. And, who eats lunch for two hours, Chandran? She's never on her desk... Don't think we aren't monitoring your behavior Sanchita."

My head was throbbing. I kept licking my dry lips and shivering. Flames of fury were dancing inside me, and my jaw was twitching from the suppressed aggression.

The senior manager held up his hand indicating Kavana to shut up. "Sanchita, you have been given the KT Sessions, isn't it? Tell me, what is the problem? Do you want more KTs?"

"No… I understood the KTs."

"Do you have a problem coming to the office early?"

"No sir—actually my house is twenty kilometers away."

"Leave your house early," he snapped. "Do you have any other concerns?" I noticed then that the other man in the suit had abandoned his laptop and was watching us keenly. Vishal maintained an impassive face while Chandran spoke.

"No—sir," I answered.

"I don't want to hear any complaints about you again," he told me. "From now on, she'll be directly under us. Her work, timings—Vishal will supervise it."

Kavana was grinning with pleasure. "Thank you, Chandran. I'll give Vishal the access details. He can monitor her directly."

"Alright then," said Chandra, rubbing his stubby hands together. "I guess we're done here. Sanchita, you may leave."

I got up, thanked them and stumbled out of the door immediately. I cursed under my breath, still clutching the medical report tightly. It felt like someone had slapped me tightly across my face. I paced to my seat wanting to hide my face as if I was a convict and had been accused of a heinous crime that I didn't want the world to know about.

"You had a meeting with Kavana?"

News spread fast. "Yes," I told Bhoomija, without looking at her.

"What did she say? Why didn't she call me?"

I got up and left. I went to the washroom and splashed some water on my face. But it didn't help. I was dying to meet Alisha and go for a walk, but I didn't want to risk it after that fiasco in the conference room. I sent Alisha a text message to ask if she would be free after work.

Alisha replied instantly that her landlord was coming home and she needed to arrange the rent by then.

"Baby, how was your trip?" Raghav texted. "Heard you're back."

I didn't know where he heard it from, but I didn't bother to ask. He wouldn't reveal his sources, and I was least interested in picking up a petty fight with him.

"It was good," I texted back with a smiley. He told me that a new Chinese restaurant had opened near his office and he was hoping to take me there this evening. I thought about it for a moment and then agreed. My hair needed shampooing I noticed on the washroom mirror on my way out. I hated tying my hair in a rubber band on dates, but I had little choice today with my oily hair. I smiled to myself as I went back to my seat. I couldn't believe I was looking forward to having dinner with Raghav.

Alisha pinged me on Lync. I told her it might be tapped and asked her to text me on my phone instead.

"Don't be ridiculous. Emails get supervised, not chat messages." Alisha sent a message on my phone.

"That bitch can tap into anything." I messaged her back.

"What happened? Did Ursula tell you that? That's against company policy. Can't employees have *any* privacy?"

"I had a meeting with Ursula. Long story. I'll tell you when we meet." I sent it quickly. After that, I lost the network connection on my phone.

"Alright. I heard there's a lot of traffic building up already." A couple of minutes later my phone beeped. Lync was so much more convenient. Nevertheless, I didn't want to get caught again.

"It's five," I messaged back. My phone beeped with the answer.

"Rain."

I looked to my left and saw a bunch of people huddled around the window on our floor whose blinds were drawn up. Nothing otherwise suggested rain. Our project bay was always the same: the slow humming of machines, clicking noises from the typing, and the blaring tube light overhead. We would never know if it were rain or shine, morning or night, or see the stars coming out at twilight. The glass too was soundproof, so if an apocalypse occurred, we would be the last ones to know.

There was a sea of vehicles outside the building at seven. Alisha had been right. I called my driver and told him to pick me up from the main gate of Ecospace. Judging by the frenzied traffic, it would take him at least two hours to get out of the campus. By then I would be back from my dinner date. It was a foolproof plan.

I walked down the lane with my heavy backpack. As the cool air hit my face, the terrible events of the day began to wear off. High-rise buildings, wet streets, and the soft orange glow of the evening lights somehow made even Ecospace a picturesque sight. Raghav was waiting for me outside the gate on his motorbike. I waved when he looked in my direction. He got off the bike and gave me a long-stemmed rose.

"How lovely," I said.

"Not lovelier than you," he said swiftly. It was a tad cheesy, but I suppose it was unintentional.

As I took it from him, a thorn brushed against my finger. I rubbed my fingers involuntarily while he bent on the bike to retrieve the extra helmet.

"Thanks," I wore the helmet and sat back. We zoomed past the jealous four-wheelers stuck in the traffic jam.

Schezwan Kitchen was situated on the ground floor of a shopping mall. It was a quaint, little restaurant whose interiors were splashed in shades of red and black. The place was dimly lit and pleasantly fragrant.

"Ni hao," said the waiter as soon as we entered. *"Theese way pleese—"*

"Authentic Chinese food," explained Raghav, as I followed the waiter to a booth on the right. Raghav walked behind me with his arm at the small of my back. "I hear the chef and staff are *actually* from China."

I nodded uncomfortably and wondered when would be a good time to tell him I didn't prefer Chinese food. "Great," I whispered, with *faux* enthusiasm.

The red leather upholstery creaked as I took my seat. "I hate when this happens. It's like you have to be embarrassed for a fart noise that didn't even come out of you."

He laughed.

"You order?" asked the waiter, bowing.

I sincerely hoped the waiter hadn't heard my comment. We scanned the menu and ordered the *manchow soup*, some deep-fried *wantons* and *Chun jûan* for starters, and *Hakka-noodles* for the main course. After nodding his head an unnecessary number of times, the waiter left.

The red paper lantern hanging low from the false ceiling lit up our faces dramatically. Raghav told me his company had clinched a new deal. And though his supervisor was in charge of the project, he would be actively handling most of the work. Raghav had always been driven when it came to his work. Until now his life had been exactly what he wanted. Sometimes, he even liked to call himself a visionary. 'One must always have a plan in hand' was his motto. Though I didn't share his enthusiasm, I wished him luck for his new project.

"How was your day?" he asked, chewing on the noodles.

"Terrible," I said between mouthfuls. The spice had begun to burn my insides. "Don't ask."

And that's when it happened. Our blissful evening came to a blistering end. He began to insist. So, I told him what had happened—the meeting and the senior manager's opinion of me.

"Sanchi, tsk, tsk," he said, shaking his head in annoyance. "This is your fault. Why did you let the situation get out of hand like this? I had told you to befriend them, approach them one by one."

I took in a deep breath. "I did engineering to develop new technology, not please people! Don't start this again."

"Don't you get it?" he said, raising a finger. "Why didn't you say anything in the meeting? You should have told them straight away that you're not assigned any work."

"It was so unexpected," I said, sipping a glass of water. "I thought she had called the meeting to screw me for bunking. I had taken the medical reports with me."

"You're such a coward," he grunted. "You never speak your mind. You don't have confidence that is the problem. Ask your friends they'll tell you—"

"I don't have confidence?" I took a deep breath to calm down. I did not want to argue. "Let's leave."

"Great, now you're mixing your professional life with your personal one," he said, casually licking the food from his fingers. "What are you doing? Sit down."

"I'm late." I left the booth.

"Now, you're running away," he called out. "So matured Sanchita!"

I closed my eyes, turned around and walked back to the booth. "For the record, I HATE Chinese food," I said and stormed out of that restaurant.

Thirteen

The next morning I was wary of Raghav's patch up gifts, but they didn't arrive. I had made up my mind to take charge of my career with all my vigor. I got dressed early and left home early. Yet, I was ten minutes late, owing to traffic. But I had a plan. This time I went straight up to the seventh floor instead of fifth. I crossed my fingers and walked inside.

"Hi," I said breathlessly when I found her desk.

"Hey!" greeted Alisha. "You're so early. What's up?"

"I'm late," I said, still panting. "Could I ask a favour of you? Don't think I'm crazy but, would you keep my bag with you today?"

Alisha regarded me as though it was the most absurd request anyone had made of her. "Sure."

"Thanks. I love you," I said and made to leave.

"Is everything okay?"

"Yes… See if I hold the bag and walk-in Ursula will again remark that I'm late. Without the bag, I can slip in through the back door and pretend like I've been there all the time."

Smirked Alisha and nodded. "Wouldn't Lync show your status as offline?"

"Logged in ten minutes ago," I said waving my cellphone at her. "You are sure I can leave my bag here? Nobody will ask you about it?"

"Not a problem at all."

"Later," I waved and ran back to the elevators. "I've got lots to tell you."

As I had expected, without my bag I did not get any disapproving stares from anyone in my project. Kavana thought I was coming back from the loo to my desk. I walked straight up to her desk as she was switching on her system and asked her to assign me some work. She wanted my interest, now that is exactly what I shall show her. I figured I would pester her to give me work until she did, ask her to teach me new things, keep telling her how keen I am to learn more modules, pretend like I am doing something of the utmost importance even when I have nothing to do as everybody else does in this building.

Of course, she was not somebody who would give in so easily; she said in a sweet voice that she would assign some incidents to me and sent me back. A couple of hours passed and as I had anticipated, she gave me nothing to do. I did not give up. I was relentless. Again, I went back to her desk with the same request. People were watching us curiously and Kavana couldn't get rid of me that easily this time. Therefore, she gave me an incident to work on and sent me shuffling to my desk. It was a menial one, which would not require more than ten minutes of my time to solve.

I knew this was the best I could get out of her for now, and so I kept quiet. Then, I pretended to take three hours to solve that incident and marked the same on my timesheet. Two could play at this game. I had decided never to mark 'idle' on the office timesheet again.

When it was time for lunch, I pinged Alisha on Lync to not to go downstairs. Instead, I ran up the stairs to the seventh floor. When she looked at me quizzically I explained to her that I had to take my lunch box out of my bag.

"Oh, I forgot," she said, still looking at me strangely. "Want to take your bag downstairs?"

"If I take it downstairs now, everyone will assume I'm going back home," I said, zipping my bag and putting it back on her desk. "These are for you, by the way."

"Ah! You remembered my chocolates," she said, taking the bag of souvenirs and Swiss chocolates from my hand.

In a secluded corner in the canteen away from the prying ears of other employees, I told Alisha about my meeting with Kavana and Chandran.

"I can't believe you didn't say anything," she said, eating watermelon from her fruit bowl. Alisha hardly ate these days. She had turned pale of late, and her collarbones were almost jutting out.

"God, how do I explain it to you? That Chandran is like an *Asura* from the *Patalaloka!"* I said in anger. "Don't laugh. Look at him and tell me you don't anticipate horns on his head. Anyway, he didn't give me a chance to speak. He went on admonishing me."

"This is not school for god sake." Said Alisha. "If Ursula's not giving you any work that's not your fault. I think you should speak to your manager alone."

"I will," I said agitatedly. "If that bitch still doesn't give me work, I'll speak to the manager."

Then I told her about what had happened with Raghav.

Alisha sighed and declared in cliché, "All men are the same."

"Don't mix your professional and personal life it seems," I said, still infuriated at his words. I cut my chapatti with deliberate force. "Who does he think he is? My family? Even my family has never said that to me."

"And what kind of a stupid statement is that? It's not like I can switch on a button and be professional. And then switch it off and be personal. I'm ONE person!" I said, chewing the piece of chapatti. "Well, guess what? It's not always butterflies and roses. If you like someone you have to share their problems too, not just their success."

"Exactly," said Alisha but she was lost in her thoughts. "And what do I get in return for sharing both? Cheated on."

"Did you know *I* filled his application form for the US?" said she, in a fit of rage. "I even wrote his SOP… Ran around to get people to sign his LOR… And what was he doing? Banging some chick from his office!"

"He's a jackass," I said, looking her in the eye. "Ali, you need to forget him."

"I've made it so easy for him. All he has to do is take his GRE and march off to the United States of America," she went on. "We had planned everything together. We had even decided to get apartments together."

"I know," I said, thinking of some way to distract her. "When are you taking the GREs?"

"The day after tomorrow," she said. "I'll not come to the office tomorrow. I'll stay at home and prepare."

"Good. Forget about everything else and study. All the best!"

After lunch, I had nothing to do. I told Kavana, and she said if anything came up, she would assign it to me. Nothing did. Ergo, an hour later I sneaked up to the office library. I opened the browser on one of the systems and searched for some writing courses on Google. I was lucky to stumble upon an online writing course and signed up for it immediately. I plugged in my earphones and began to watch. A celebrated international author, all the way from his home in New Zealand was teaching the course. I hadn't heard of him nor read any of his books, but made it a point to look for it in the bookstore next time. I found his mannerisms amicable and his lessons easy to follow. It amazed me how easy it was. One could learn anything from the comfort of their home thanks to the Internet. One moment I was wishing to be a writer, and the next moment this course had materialized at my fingertips. Could it be true that what we seek is seeking us? Anyway, I didn't want to jinx it with my doubts. So I quickly watched a couple of lessons more before going back to my desk on the fifth floor.

On my way home that day, I thought about the assignment I had to do for the writing class and my mind hardly noticed the traffic.

The next two days Kavana gave me no work, no matter how many times I asked her for it.

"Do you think I should speak to the manager?" I asked Alisha over a text message. She had finished her GREs and was getting out of the exam centre.

"YES!" she sent back.

'I will," I texted back.

Bhoomija was browsing some Indian history pages on her system. Peculiar… But, I didn't ask her. She had told me long ago that social studies had been her favourite subject in school. I wondered if she also didn't have any incidents to work on.

I sent another message. "But, I don't know how to. I've never spoken to him. He sits alone in a cabin."

"Ping him on Lync," she sent with a rolling eyes emoticon.

"Yes, I can do that. How was the exam?"

"Not as good as I had expected. Nonetheless, not too bad either."

"You're being modest. Wish me luck."

"You don't need luck. Go. Kick some ass."

"Pinging him. Bye."

I opened my Lync messenger and searched for Vishal. He was online, but as I pinged him, his Lync status changed to 'Away.'

ME: Hello, sir.

VISHAL: Hi, Sanchita.

To my amazement, he replied instantly.

ME: I wanted to speak to you.

ME: I had some concerns. Please tell me when to meet you?

I waited for a while, but I didn't get any reply.

An hour later,

VISHAL: Please come to my cabin.

VISHAL: I presume you know where it is?

ME: Yes I do. I will be there.

When I entered Vishal's cabin who should greet me, but Kavana? I froze at the door looking at the sight of Vishal, Chandran and the man in the suit sitting on one side of the table as if they were gathered to interview me. I felt deceived once again. So, the idiot had taken one hour to gather them?

"Come in, Sanchita," greeted Vishal.

Kavana was pacing the length of the room behind the three men. The smirk on her face enraged me further. It was as if she was silently challenging me. Did Vishal need an army of men to speak to a mere employee? Was he a sum of three and not an individual? To top it all he had even invited Kavana.

I hesitated, but for a moment. I wanted to wipe that smile off Kavana's face, with a mace. But the only weapons I had were my words. And I was going to use them.

"Hi Vishal," I said, looking straight at him and ignoring the others in the room. I had come to speak to him and I would.

"Yes Sanchita," he said, calmly. "Please tell me your concerns."

"Let me tell you from the beginning. I joined Global Software Services in July, last year. I was selected through campus placements. And, I was overjoyed. I was a Distinction holder in college and my grade points never dropped below 9 GPA. You can verify the records," I said without breaking eye contact with him. He nodded. "So, I joined this company on the twenty-eighth of July last year. I underwent basic training for twenty days. I was then placed in the domain training under the Enterprise Management module. My training was completed in September and after clearing the training exams, I joined the Popshake project on the twenty-third of that month along with a colleague, Bhoomija. I was in the Shadow period for a month during which I received KTs in the Enterprise Management module. By November, I was told," I looked at Kavana for a moment, with fire in my eyes. I despised the woman. She had stopped pacing mid-way and stood behind Vishal. "I was told I would be assigned incidents in the same module and would be allowed to work independently. Instead, what transpired was something different. Kavana came up to me in November and told me that Bhoomija and I would be shifted to another module, CRM, as she required more people in that team. I told her that I had never learnt that module. She assured me that it would be taught. So, I happily agreed. And the KT period began again in December. Tarun gave some presentations on the theory part of the module, which we have to date never used while solving real-time problems in the module. Yet, within a month, by January of this year, I was working independently on the CRM module incidents. Why was I suddenly asked not to work on anything from February?"

Kavana was holding the back of Vishal's chair. She was staring at me with tear-filled eyes. It was the rage. She looked like a psychopath ready to strike. The smile on her face had now been completely wiped off. I scowled at her and went on.

"I was not given any work in February, March, and April, despite my persistent requests. I would like to know the reason for this. Why is it that Bhoomija is being given all the work and I am not?"

Vishal still had an impassive expression on his face.

"Kavana?" asked Vishal, who had now seated herself beside the suited man. "You want to answer this?"

I could almost see smoke coming out of her nostrils.

"I was trying to map her to a more technical team," she gulped. "S—Since she was from a Computer Science background, I figured she likes core technology and as her lead, it is my duty to map her to her interests. So that she is more enthusiastic about her work."

"Even now, I have asked numerous times to be assigned some work," I said, still addressing Vishal. I had gone there to speak to him, and so I kept my focus on him. I had no interest in fighting with this woman. "Why am I not being given any work? Without it how will I progress in this company? I'm highly *enthusiastic* about my work," I emphasized the word giving Kavana a sideways glance, "and would like to know how to improve upon my current situation so that I am a good resource for Popshake and in turn for Global Software Services? And if there isn't any work here for me, would I at least be rolled off this project?"

"Enough," bellowed Chandran; butting-in conversations where he was not invited to was his talent. "We do not allow employees to tell on their bosses!"

Kavana was squirming and turning in her seat. She was staring at me with abhorrence. A hint of a smile touched my lips. *Challenge me again, bitch!* Vishal was looking at Kavana, waiting for her to say something.

"She's never on time to the office," Kavana had finally found her voice.

"But why isn't she being given any work Kavana?" asked Vishal. I felt like my mission was accomplished.

"You don't understand. She's always late. She's never on her desk." Kavana was feeling the heat. "From now on she will be assigned more incidents as and when they come up."

"You should be glad you're being given this liberty to come and talk to us… Complaining on your boss like this. It does not reflect well on your character, believe me," said Chandran to me. Was Chandran stooping so low as to threaten me now?

"Chandran, may I handle this please?" asked Vishal. Chandran swished his hand dramatically in the air and pushed back in his seat. "Thank you."

He does not require the support of his army to speak now? I thought sarcastically.

"Sanchita," said Vishal, drawing my attention. He was wearing the same impassive look as before. "I see great potential for you in Popshake."

I gaped. Had this douchebag heard nothing? How does not doing any work show great potential? I came to him with a crisis.

"Let me assure you, you are doing splendidly. I see a bright future for you at Global Software Services. And as for your course of action—Kavana is your lead, your supervisor. She's here to guide you. Continue to follow her instructions and she will help you out."

What the hell?

"Have I addressed your concerns? Do you have anything more to share?"

"Yes—and no, I have nothing more to share."

"Very well then," he said with a skilled smile. "You may leave."

"Thank you," I got up and left.

Coming out of the glass door of the cabin, I felt like a celebrity. I had opened my mouth and how! The cool air of the air conditioning hit my face and made my hair fly like in the movies. I felt thrilled. Thrilled that I had spoken my mind and accomplished what I had set out to do. I'll bet Kavana had not expected it. I had seen the shock on her face, and it satisfied me. In my mental match of challenges against Kavana, we were now: one all.

Fourteen

Bhoomija pounced on me as soon as I came to the office the next day.

"Come here," she said, pulling me to the break out area.

"Let me log in at least," I said, breaking free of her grasp. Then, I followed her to the break out area.

"I heard you spoke to the manager yesterday," she whispered, breathlessly.

Should've expected.

"Yes," I was unsure how much information I should divulge to her. Now I came to know why people had stared at me weirdly when I came to the office that morning.

"You complained about Kavana to Vishal?"

"I didn't complain per se," I said, carefully. "I asked what I must do if—"

"Awesome!" She squealed in joy. "That's brilliant. You have so much guts dude," she said patting my back.

I raised an eyebrow. "*You* are saying this?"

"I wish I had done it. Kavana is a big jackass."

It was the first time I had heard that word coming from her and it sounded rather funny when she said it. "I'm sorry, did I hear that right?" I asked shaking my head.

"She's a chameleon. One minute she tells you she's going to make you the head—gives you hopes, colourful dreams, and lift you high. And the next minute she throws you down the drain—telling you you're a worthless parasite."

"What happened? Did she say something to you?"

"Why will she say anything to me? I will tell her. She's the most useless person here. After Tarun left I have been solving incidents here. One of the issues was taking some time and the client was acting impatient. Instead of asking the client to wait, she scolded me so much. I wanted to ask her if she was so smart why doesn't she solve it herself?"

"She can't," I chuckled.

"I know she can't. She doesn't know the A, B, C of systems. Don't know who made her a lead. All she can do is sit on her desk and play with our careers! She wants to use us as pawns and throw us out whenever she feels like it."

I couldn't believe what I was hearing. Should nod in agreement with Bhoomija or stay silent? What if she bitched about me to Kavana when she was feeling better? Still, I was impressed Bhoomija had ultimately understood Kavana and she was stating it so blatantly.

"Hush, if anybody walks in..." I looked over my shoulder. She was drinking her green tea. "You want some?"

"No thanks," I shook my head. I drank a glass of water and both of us walked out. The rest of the day, people kept staring at me and whispering. From a 'who-is-that-rich-girl-in-the-office' I had suddenly become a 'watch-out-for-her-she-is-dangerous.' I was their new hero. A couple of more people asked me if I had told on my boss and even congratulated me. I naïvely rejoiced in the newfound fandom, unaware that I had dug my own grave.

*

My phone rang when I was having lunch with Alisha. I didn't pick it. Raghav had tried reaching out to me four times from morning. His text messages read as if nothing had happened between us.

Alisha told me she ran into Deepak at the GRE centre. It was awkward and heartbreaking. Later, he had gone back to her place to pick up some of his stuff.

"He wanted his favourite shirt back," said Alisha. "I wanted to cut it to shreds in front of his eyes."

"Did you?"

"No."

"Would've served him right."

"He's not worth it. I gave him his shirt back and he left. He's not worth my anger or my revenge."

My phone rang again.

"Raghav?" said Alisha. I nodded.

"I must break up with him." She nodded. I cut the call and sent him a text message.

"Meet me at 4, Starbucks."

Raghav arrived on the dot. It was a sunny day. We took a table upstairs in the crowded café. In his stark white shirt and grey flannels, Raghav was looking debonair. He had rolled up his sleeves and even gelled his hair. I tried to capture a mental image. I knew we would never meet again. I waited for him to finish his cappuccino and then said it all in a flurry.

"Why are you doing this Sanchita?" He demanded through gritted teeth, his cool composure from earlier had slipped. "Is it because we fought the other day?"

He held my hands in a vise-like grip.

"No, it's not because we fought," I said. People from the neighbouring tables were watching us. But, I knew I had to do it. "Please don't make this hard for me."

"You're making it impossible for me." He yelled, tightening his grip. "Can't we work through this?"

I shook my head. "I'm sorry."

Suddenly, he loosened his grip on me and considered me with cold eyes.

"I should leave," I said, my voice was shaking. I got up. "Drive safely. Don't think about—"

"Just go."

I turned, walked downstairs and went out of the restaurant, without turning back. My heart was still hammering in my throat and a teardrop slid down my cheek as I walked back to Ecospace.

When I returned that evening I was welcomed by two shocking events.

Bhoomija was browsing Indian history on her computer again: Indus Valley civilization, and Ajanta, Ellora Caves.

"Where did you go? I wanted to have coffee with you," she said as soon as she saw me.

"Sorry, I had mine," I replied. I was skeptical as to why I was being subjected to this sudden outburst of love from Bhoomija.

"I wanted to tell you something," she said. "I've decided to put down my papers,"

I didn't know if she was joking, but I wanted to do a cartwheel in the middle of the office floor.

"How come all of a sudden?" I ventured out, to make sure she wasn't joking. When I was wondering how to fix the problem, the problem itself was walking out. I couldn't believe my luck.

"I'm sick of this corporate world. You have to dress a certain way, behave in a certain manner. People judge you by your appearance all the time. It's exhausting," she said. "In my village, people don't stop talking to me when I oil my hair."

"Do you know what I really want?" she said, pulling me close. She didn't care who was looking at us in the bay. Her eyes shone with zest. "I want to be able to oil my hair, braid it, wear a salwar kameez and pin a dupatta to it." She made a hand gesture in the form of a V around her neck indicating how she would pin her the dupatta.

What a strange desire, I thought.

"That is the real me," she emphasized. "I want to be free. I want to be myself again."

"You want to go back to your village?" I had no idea one's dream could be that simple.

"Yes," she said. "I haven't even told my parents yet. They would be delighted if I left the city and moved back. But, I wanted to ask you before that… Do you think I'm making the right choice?"

With her out of the picture, Kavana would have no choice but to give me the promotion.

"Yes. Absolutely," I said, hoping I didn't sound too eager. If she could steal my work, I could let her make some bad decisions. "Do what you feel like."

"Thanks," she said and suddenly pulled me into a hug. "I knew you would understand." I thought she was crazy.

The second shock greeted me a couple of hours later, when I was on my way home, stuck in traffic somewhere near Koramangala.

"Babe, I got back with Dee."

"ARE YOU FUCKING OUT OF YOUR MIND?" I replied to Alisha's text message. And then, I realized Deepak might be next to her and looking at her phone. How could one forgive someone who had cheated on them? Had she lost it?

*

My little stint had led to a cold war between us. Kavana did not miss an opportunity to breathe down my neck. I had to hide wherever I went. I felt more like a backyard thief than an employee. If she spotted me going to the loo she would send me a warning mail. She would also tag the manager in it! If she found me in the canteen, mails would be sent to the demon god, *Asura*, also known as Chandran. Meanwhile, the work she assigned to me was still insufficient.

Alisha dismissed me when I lamented to her. It was bound to happen after that meeting I had called.

Kavana was shocked to find out that her beloved disciple, Bhoomija was resigning from the company. She tried to stop her, but Bhoomija was firm in her decision. Bhoomija even offered to pay the compensation amount for an early resignation without a notice period. She wanted to take up the civil services examination and pursue a career in the government administration departments. She wanted to chase her dreams at lightning speed. The haste with which she wanted to run from here surprised me. I didn't know whether to call her foolish or a genius.

I, on the other hand, was falling into depression. By the time I realized it, I had been immersed neck-deep in its deadly waters. These waters seemed tranquil to any onlooker. Little did they know the water was poisoned, eating me from the inside bit by bit. I felt like I carried a weight on my chest all the time. It was present in every smile, every scowl, every laugh, and every howl.

The weight never left me alone. My life had become so monotonous. There was nothing I looked forward to.

I would wake up in the morning and get ready for the office. After spending about two hours in traffic, yelling and grunting at every passing vehicle, I would reach the office. I would rush to the elevators and consider myself the luckiest if I found one immediately, lest my shift hours in the office would not be complete. I would run out of the elevator doors, hiding my bag otherwise everyone might know how late I was to office. I would first go upstairs to my best friend's project and keep my bag in her place, and then come down to my floor and sneak into my project, pretending I was there all along. Some days, I genuinely tried to wake up early and leave my home, and whenever I was successful in the first two steps, I'd surely end up in traffic. Later, I became too disinterested in the life that I was living that waking up did not seem like a priority.

"Tell me honestly why did you break up with him?" Alisha asked me one day when we were sitting under our beloved berry tree. "Apart from the fact that he was nagging you and judging you..."

Alisha was under the impression that my depression was because of my break-up. Despite my warnings, she had tried to set me up with two of her friends.

I took a deep breath and exhaled. "…I was not in love with him."

"Ah," she said, hugging me. "I think you did the right thing then. And don't worry, you'll meet the love of your life soon."

"No thank you," I said, pushing her away. "I've told you I don't need anyone. I'm happy to be on my own."

Then she told me she wished she could've been more like me. Alisha was not able to get over Deepak no matter how hard she tried. And when Deepak had shown up on her door front, half-drunk, and begging for her to take him back, she hadn't been able to refuse. They had been together for five years, and she was still in love with him.

But, I was lost in thoughts concerning me. How many more years would I sit in front of the same computer, under that headache-causing tube light in a 5-by-5" foot space? I didn't even have a cubicle to myself, let alone a cabin. I would rather kill myself than sit there for the next twenty to fifty years, living the same day over and over again. I swear I had not thought of this when I took up engineering. I often found myself wondering what would happen if I dropped dead. I mused myself in the answer: it would all come to an end then. I knew these were passive suicidal thoughts. Harmless. I would never act upon them until one night. I was suffering from sleeplessness, crying into my pillow and I tried suffocating myself to death with it. I stopped in the act, and immediately went into the bathroom and splashed some water on my face. Was I going to die for Global Software Services? Would it even matter to them if I did? The idea seemed bonkers to me. I laughed at my reflection in the mirror. I was going mad. And I desperately wanted to save myself. Hence, I bunked office the next day and went to a psychologist, without telling anybody.

I knew the psychologist. She was my old school teacher. I waited in the lobby while the door to her office opened and a slender girl of not more than fifteen years of age walked out, swaying a lunch bag in her hand. I had heard from some of my friends that they used to discuss their relationship problems with this teacher back in high school. I wondered if this girl was here for a similar reason. That gave me a bit of confidence to speak my mind.

"Come in," called out the psychologist. She had not aged at all from when I had last seen her. She had the same blackish-grey hair, rimmed glasses and a soft smile on her complacent face. After the formal greeting, I apologized to her for not making an appointment and thanked her for seeing me. She said she did not have much time as the next client would arrive soon, but she would see me, as I was an old student of hers. I don't think she recognized me though, and I was quite glad.

"So, what is the problem?" she asked me straight away, as I sat fidgeting. "You are here for a reason, I believe?"

"It's my work," I said, breathing heavily. I narrated the events that had taken place in the office. I avoided telling her anything about my love life or my depression. Nothing good came out of our meeting though. After listening to me for twenty minutes, she told me to quit my job. I told her that was not an option. I didn't have another job offer in hand and I hadn't struggled through engineering for four years to stay at home. She then asked me about my salary. When I told her, she laughed. She asked me to become a nursery teacher or do some gardening.

"Pardon me, but it is not like you're earning millions. If you were, I would have told you to put up with nonsense—at least you are making money. But, you're not. Do you see any point in struggling like this?"

I was livid, but I didn't show it. A minute later, she made it clear that she wanted me to leave. So I did. She didn't ask me to meet her again. When I came out of her office I was so irritated, and on a whim, I dialed Nishant.

"You mean like college days?" he asked when I asked him to bunk his office and meet me. I laughed. We had so many fond memories of bunking college together. "Alright, when my boss goes to the loo, I'll take my bag and sneak out!"

He met me in Koramangala an hour later. We watched a Hindi movie in *PVR Cinemas* in Forum Mall like old times and headed out to a close-by bar afterward. I felt so good when I spent time with him. Nishant was better for my mental health than the psychologist. *Boozy Fish* was a trendy bar that hosted live concerts on Thursday nights. Nishant told me he frequented this place.

"Why can't it be like this every day?" I asked Nishant while we ate.

"If you meet me, it will," he said winking at me.

I told him about my meeting with the psychologist. "I don't know what I was expecting to hear when I went there. Do you know what I truly wish? I wish I could be a writer. Maybe I wanted her to say it to me. I don't know. But all I truly want to do is write. Write about people, places, and life. It's what I have wanted to do from when I was eleven years old."

"Really?" he asked, frankly surprised. It occurred to me then that I had never shared that story with him. "You wanted to be a writer when you were eleven?"

"I wrote a book with my friend in primary school. It was not published. But, it was a good hundred pages long. We had it printed and spiral bound from a cyber shop near school. We had even made a cover image for it, all by ourselves—a blue background and a ship!" I said cheerfully. He was listening keenly. I noted he wasn't skeptical like Chetan had been when I had blurted it out to him.

"I would love to see it!" he said.

"Me too," I sighed. "I don't have it with me. It was kept in the school library. I did think a couple of times to go back there and ask for it. But, it was eleven years ago. They would not have it."

He nodded slowly. "And, to think at eleven all I wanted to be was a *Pokémon Master!*"

A band got on the stage and did a soundcheck. 'The Firecrackers' were a team of four—a drummer, bass guitarist, lead guitarist, and a singer. A stunning singer! She was slender with long legs, dusky complexion, and silky hair. She wore a mauve bandage dress that complimented her features well. I had a hunch I had seen her before. I saw Nishant watching her.

"Wasn't this the same band that played in the Italian place where we last met?" I said.

"Yes!" said Nishant, eagerly. "I knew they were playing here tonight. That's why I brought you here."

"You like them that much?" I was suspicious.

"Wait till you hear them," he said, pulling me to the dance floor. They played their first song and the crowd was under their spell. We were close to the stage, and Nishant hadn't taken his eyes off the singer. When she started singing the next song, he cheered loudly. I don't know why this irritated me, but it did. The fact that her voice was so mellifluous was not helping.

"That's an original!" yelled Nishant. "Never thought The Firecrackers would play originals so soon. They are a fairly new band…" He cheered more loudly. This time, the singer looked at us. I wanted to run away. I told him we should get out, but he said he wanted to stay for one more song. The band paused for a short break. And to my utter displeasure, the singer got off the stage and directly came up to us.

"Lekha," she said, introducing herself. "You are from R. R. Institute of Technology, aren't you?"

"Yes," we said in unison. That's where I had seen her.

"What a pleasure!" she said, shaking our hands.

"Hey, you come to all our shows, don't you?" she nudged Nishant on his arm as if she was his childhood friend. A little too amicable for a celebrity, I thought and rolled my eyes.

"Big fan," he said. "You guys are awesome."

"Sorry, I *gotta* go," she said, as one of the guitarists called her name. "But, you guys should join us backstage after the show."

"Here, take these. Show them to the bouncers and they'll let you backstage," she said with a huge smile.

"No, I don't think—"

"Of course, we will." Nishant took the passes and said to her retreating figure. "Thank you so much."

Before I could pull Nishant out, they started to play another song. And Nishant went close to the stage again. I couldn't take it anymore. I badly wanted to know if he had a crush on Lekha. I was his best friend, and I wasn't supposed to feel this way about his crushes. He was always happy for me when I had a crush back in college. Or, was he so good at pretending?

"She's beautiful, isn't she?" I asked him when he was busy hooting. "Who?"

"Lekha!" He was looking at her throughout, what did he mean 'who?'

"Are you *jealous?"* he asked, suddenly turning me around.

"Certainly not!" I snapped.

"Now it all makes sense…" he chuckled. "Why you wanted to leave… why you were acting weird around her…"

"Get lost!" I said and stormed out of the bar.

"I was cheering for the drummer actually… if it makes you feel any better," he said, following me out into the night. "Always found drums fascinating. I wanted to play—but never mind."

"Why not? You should play!" I said changing the topic. I was embarrassed to have mistaken his interest in drums for a crush on Lekha.

"But you were jealous—" he teased.

"I—wanted to leave because it was getting late. You can date Lekha for all I care!" I said, a little too loudly. And he laughed.

"But why don't you want to learn the drums?"

"I checked around—A decent drum set costs nearly twenty thousand—I tried saving up but it's never enough. And I can't ask my parents to invest in some musical instrument that I don't even know how to play…"

"Come with me," I pulled him. He waved the backstage pass at me. "But—how will I get a date with Lekha if I don't ask her out?"

"Shut up, I'm serious—" I had an idea. I had never done anything on an impulse and it was rather thrilling. I had seen a musical instruments shop in Koramangala one evening while coming back from the office. It was a few blocks up the lane, and we reached in time. We stepped inside, as the storekeeper was about to pull the shutters down.

"Sorry we're closed," said the storekeeper.

"Just one purchase," I said. "We won't take more than five minutes." Nishant was still gaping at me. The storekeeper reluctantly switched on the lights.

"We're looking for some good drums please," I said in a hurry. I had never shopped for musical instruments before and, looking at the storekeeper snigger I realized I might have sounded foolish.

"Acoustic, five-piece set," said Nishant. "In the starting range." Nishant checked the instrument. I could see the happiness in his eyes as he struck it. A shrill sound vibrated the small store.

"Shall I book it then? It's twenty-two thousand rupees. We'll deliver it to you on your doorstep in three days," he went to get a register. "Fill this form, and pay the amount."

"No—" Nishant stopped me. "It's too much. I can't accept this. Why are you doing this?"

"Because, I know the cost of a lost dream," I yelled when he wouldn't listen to me. "Besides, I've saved up enough. You can return the money later—but I want you to start learning it right away."

"I will," he said, slowly taking my hand. "I promise."

Fifteen

The hot news of the week was that Kavana was going to be rolled out of the project. One couldn't say if it was the demand of the project or because of my stint. I would like to believe it was the latter.

It was Bhoomija's last day. I bought a carrot cake with vanilla frosting on it from *au Bon Pain café* for her farewell and we set it up in the break out area.

Bhoomija pulled me to a restaurant for lunch and treated me. She was leaving and I had mixed feelings. I decided to let everything go and pulled her into a tight hug. I was going to miss her badly. And then, she apologized to me.

"Sorry I put my name on those incidents," she said. "I was so blinded by greed. I couldn't see through Kavana… And treated you wrong."

"Corporate changes us sometimes," I said. Hadn't I wanted her out of the picture for a promotion? "Listen, I did something wrong as well. I gave you some bad advice. Don't leave the company. There's still time. You can withdraw your resignation. Kavana wouldn't mind; she loves you!"

She smiled and shook her head. "Dude, I have to go. But you must do well here. You're strong and confident. I know you will handle it. But, stay cautious of Kavana. Don't fall for her tricks. Chetan's a crack, but he's not so bad. That reminds me, I haven't told him I'm leaving. He'll be pleased to know somebody finally took his advice!"

I wished her luck for the civil services examinations. She was going to study at a learning centre in Hyderabad. I told her when she visits Bangalore she must stay at my house.

The farewell was an emotional affair for Bhoomija and me. Everyone else had come for the cake. Some of them didn't even know Bhoomija. We recollected some good times and she cut the cake. Bhoomija had predicted correctly: Chetan was ecstatic that at least somebody had taken his advice.

After the farewell, Kavana pulled me back. "Mark my word," she threatened. "Your days in this office are numbered." I did not pay any heed to her.

After Bhoomija left, the burden of the entire module fell on my shoulders. But I managed it. Whenever I had any free time, I wrote stories for my writing course assignment. Depression was still weighing me down.

Alisha came crying to the office today. She had been miserable for the past few months. Deepak had been blaming her for everything. The two of them fought daily. Last night they attended his office party, where he got drunk and ridiculed her in front of his colleagues. When she asked him the reason for it on the way home after the party, he told her she was the cause of his professional failures. She had not shared all of this with me until today. This morning she had kicked him out of her house.

"You know," I said, watching the vehicles drive by. We sat on the kerb under the berry tree after lunch. "When it comes to love nothing is black or white. I think it's all grey!"

"So," she asked, cautiously, "You don't think I'm stupid?"

I knew she was referring to the relapse phase with her ex-boyfriend. "No," I said, frankly. I had stopped judging her. It could've happened to anybody. "Everybody is entitled to make a few bad decisions once in a while. I believe our mistakes are what push us in the right direction."

"Shall we celebrate our newfound singledom then?" asked Alisha. "Get drunk?"

"How about we mourn our breakups instead?" I suggested. "With buckets of chocolate ice creams and watch some 'rom-coms' in our pajamas."

"Sounds like a plan."

We sat on her bed and watched the Hollywood film, *Serendipity* that evening after office. The next day was the most anticipated time of the year for all employees: the performance cycle ratings.

In Popshake, we were asked to meet Kavana one by one in a conference room, where our ratings were disclosed to us, secretly. But the moment one came out of the conference room, the rating wasn't a secret anymore.

"Average," sighed Alisha, as we sat down for lunch in a corner table in the canteen. "She made me slog for a year and a half and she won't even promote me. What about you?"

"Below average," I said. My result had come as a complete shock to me.

"What the fuck? That's not fair. That's a rating given to people who don't even come to the office—she made you work so much these past few months."

"They give me this rating after Vishal assured me that my future in Popshake is bright…*I see a lot of potential,"* I yelled, imitating him. *"His ass he sees potential!* I didn't expect her to give me an 'employee-of-the-year' award. But, at least an average-"

"Hi," someone tapped on Alisha's shoulder. It was one of our training friends.

"Congratulations! So, where are having the promotion parties tonight?"

Alisha embarrassedly explained that she wasn't promoted. The other girl looked at her with pity. Then she made an excuse and left hastily. The scenario repeated a couple of times as more known faces entered the canteen and came up to us. We saw a guy ordering *Gulab Jamoon* for ten people to celebrate his success.

"Are we the only people in this company who aren't promoted?" asked Alisha in irritation. I suggested we go out for a walk on the campus.

"I miss school," I told her as we walked. "It was so simple back then. You study, you write the exam, and you get marks. But now, your results are not in your hands."

"I swear. The points are for ass-licking," Alisha grunted in rage. "I haven't even got my college admits for the USA. What am I going to do?"

As we turned the corner, we saw some employees cursing animatedly in the smoke zone. Kavana called me on my cellphone and I had to rush back upstairs for a meeting.

What now? Hadn't she screwed my life enough?

I had a feeling of déjà vu as I walked into the conference room. It had the grim setting as the previous times. But today, there was another woman in the room along with Kavana, Vishal, Chandran, and the suited man. She began the meet as soon as I entered.

"Hello Sanchita," she said. "I gather your performance rating has been disclosed to you."

I nodded.

"Since you have been given the below-average rating, we will be putting you in a performance improvement cycle. It's a standard procedure of the company to help underperforming employees," she said when I looked at her with surprise. My heart was hammering in my chest. I wanted to strangle Kavana. "You will be under strict supervision for a month, during which you will be assigned a set of tasks. On completion of all the tasks, you will continue to remain an employee of Global Software Services. You will not be promoted and there will be no change in your rating after the cycle. However, if you fail to complete the tasks, you will be asked to leave the company at the end of the month. This should not come to you as a surprise. You will be asked to return your ID card, tag, and other credentials. So kindly carry them with you on the result day."

I was gaping at her. Kavana was going to fire me. *Fuck!*

"As your HR, I must remind all of you that whatever has been discussed here will not leave this room. Have I made myself clear? Good. Good luck Sanchita. We will meet again at the end of the cycle."

My legs were shaking as I walked out of the conference room. I was going to be fired! I knew what my parents would say if they heard. This would be equivalent to failing a year at school.

I couldn't give up so easily. All was not lost. I would complete those bloody tasks. There was a ninety percent chance Kavana would fire me despite clearing the tasks. I studied every night. I worked hard to finish four months of work that was dumped on me, in one month. At the end of the month, I was winning. There were a few tasks undone. I was feeling sick looking at the screen for hours, so I pushed my keyboard aside and took a deep breath.

Somebody had rolled up the curtains. I looked out the glass window of our floor and caught a glimpse of the outside world. A new building was being constructed opposite ours inside the campus. I noticed a laborer laying bricks. Unintentionally, I observed him for a while and an odd thought struck me. We were exactly like one another. We worked for some hours daily and got our wages. At least he knew what he was building when he laid those bricks: a wall. I didn't even know that. The worst part was I didn't even have the desire to know where my work would fit in the big picture of the company. Why had I taken up engineering in the first place? Was it because everyone else was doing it, or had I chosen it out of sheer greed?

My screen blinked and I turned my attention to it. My heart froze. I had received feedback from the New Zealand author for my assignments in the writing course. I covered my mouth as I read it in a hurry. I wanted to scream. My eyes filled up. A colleague, who sat next to me, asked if I was okay? I nodded. I had never felt this thrilled about my work in the company, not even when I had received my first paycheck.

I completed the rest of the tasks and left. I didn't know if I would see my desk again, and so I wanted to take all my belongings. Then I saw that there was nothing there that belonged to me. It was as if I had never occupied this space.

*

Nishant enrolled himself in a music class on the day that the drums were delivered to him. He had been practicing promptly after work. He told me it was the part of the day that he looked forward to the most and no matter how demanding his job had become he never skipped his drum-time.

We attended a few more concerts of The Firecrackers and caught up with them backstage at times. They were working professionals who practiced on the weekends and played for the crowds on Fridays. The lead guitarist and bassist were accountant and marketing manager, while the drummer and Lekha worked as engineers for a multinational company.

A month later, a perfect opportunity presented itself to Nishant. The drummer of The Firecrackers was moving out, as he was being sent to London from his company, for an onshore project. Nishant asked if he could replace him in the band and The Firecrackers were more than happy to welcome him. What fun it was to watch him play. His brothers and sisters too had joined us for one of the concerts when they had come to Bangalore during the Christmas vacations. They jested that they had a rock-star in the family and were so proud of Nishant. I never missed any of his concerts at least until I received my performance rating at the office. I hadn't met him for a month now, and I missed him terribly. I was going to tell him today. I had butterflies in my stomach at the thought of it.

The Firecrackers were tremendously successful. After playing at various bars and restaurants in Bangalore, they were selected for an international music festival in Hong Kong. It was Nishant's first trip out of the country and he was continuously sending me pictures from the past four days: the cobblestone alleys, *Madame Tussauds*, and the stadium where the competition was held. Unfortunately, they had lost by a whisker, and Lekha was a tad disappointed. He had updated me last night.

A strange feeling had troubled me and brought me to the airport this evening. What if he was dating Lekha? After all, they were on a trip together in a romantic city. My phone started ringing. He had landed. I told him the café in which I sat.

"Why did you want to see me in such a hurry?" he asked, dropping his backpack onto the floor to give me a hug.

"I—I was passing by—" In retrospect, my actions were beginning to seem a little foolish to me.

"You were *passing* by the airport?" he was considering me keenly. "What is it?"

I decided to come right out and say it. "I think you know what is it," I said. A slow smile touched his lips and he waited for me to go on. "I love you."

"Sorry? What was that?"

"I said I love you," I said a little more loudly. Suddenly, he stopped grinning.

"And you just assumed I was not dating anyone?" he asked raising an eyebrow. My mouth fell open. Lekha had come to our table. Both of them exchanged a knowing look. I was still gaping. I wished I hadn't said anything.

"I'm kidding," he said, bursting into a laugh. "I love you too, stupid. I tried to tell you on the last day of college, but—"

"Shut up, I'll kill you!" I was beating him with my purse.

Lekha joined in the laughter. "I'm so happy for you guys," she said pulling us into a hug. Then, she joined the rest of The Firecrackers in the front, giving us a moment to hug and kiss.

"I quit my job today," I told Nishant after we sat down again. Unbelievable as it may sound, I had passed the performance improvement cycle. Yet, I had decided to quit.

"Why?" he asked.

"It was making me unhappy," I told him.

"Best decision ever. I have something for you by the way," he said, reaching into his backpack. He gave me some chocolates and a curio. "Wait, there's one more thing."

A blue spiral-bound copy with an amateur cover image, perhaps created by eleven-year-olds was placed on the coffee table.

Epilogue

"Parents, relatives, neighbours, friends and my friends' parents, the same people who had showered me with praises when I had secured my first job as a software engineer, now looked upon me with distaste. I was no longer living my life by their standard. My friend's parents were worried to let their kids near me as if my choices were contagious. I was being treated like an outcast. My parents, on the other hand, behaved as if I was dying and an MBA, a Master of Science degree in a foreign country, or a Java course was like an oxygen mask that they were desperately trying to throw at me."

The crowd laughed when I said it. I was standing on a small podium of a bookshop I had frequented as a child.

"Sometimes, people feel threatened by someone who dares to follow their heart. It means that they could've done the same, if they weren't too scared or lazy. And that's not what they want to hear. But don't let their opinions dictate your way of life. If you have a dream, don't be afraid to chase it."

I saw Nishant entering the shop along with Alisha. I smiled. I had introduced them to each other a year ago. Alisha had moved to the United States to pursue a post-graduation degree in machine learning in San Diego. We spoke to each other over Skype on weekends. Alisha lived in a flat close to her university, had learnt a little bit of cooking and had trimmed her hair to her ears.

I hadn't seen Bhoomija either for a year. But we kept in touch. We spoke once a month. She didn't have the time. The learning centre in Hyderabad strictly prohibited the use of social media and had signal blockers in place. But as a consequence of that, Bhoomija had done exceptionally well in the main exams. She had cleared the first round with flying colours, and she was now preparing for the interview round. She was delighted to hear that I had written a novel, and despite her tight schedule, she had instantly made plans to come down for the launch. I waved to her as she entered. She smiled and showed me a thumbs-up. Then, she spotted Alisha at the far end, amid the crammed bookshelves and joined her.

"You may win, or you may lose. You will not know unless you take a step forward in the direction of your dreams. In the end, it is never about success or failure, it is about doing something that brings you joy."

I wrapped up my speech and got off the stage amidst warm applause.

The weight on my chest had disappeared. Though grief made a brief appearance now and then, I could safely say depression had left my system. I felt liberated.

Nishant walked up to me after the crowd had cleared.

"May I borrow the author for a lunch date?" he whispered, running his finger through the length of my hair.

"Only a moment," I smiled and disappeared behind the bookshelves.

I picked up a paperback copy of my beloved author from the fiction section and joined the three of them at the counter. We held hands as we crossed the street across the bookstore. It was a bright, pleasant day in Bangalore with a slight chance of rainfall.

The End

Acknowledgments

I would like to express my heartfelt gratitude to,

My grandfather Srinivas B. Sawkar, for instilling a love of language and stories in me.

Soumya P. Sawkar, my little sister, for being my in-house grammarian, first reader, proofreader, and what-not.

My grandmother Pramila S. Sawkar, my father Pradeep S. Sawkar and my mother Sujata P. Sawkar for everything.

Mr. Anuj Kumar and the entire team of Kalamos Literary Services for bringing this book into the world and making my dream come true.

Mr. Chhimi Tenduf-La, the renowned author, for his guidance, handy tips, and for believing in my story when I was about to give up.

Darshan, Shweta, Anushree, Navya, Sneha, Subhashree, and all my friends for handling my dramas in real life, so I can handle them on the page; also, for being my constant source of love, support, and laughter.

Lastly, but most importantly, my readers, for loving my tales and inspiring me to spin some more.

About The Author

Shalini P Sawkar is an Indian Author of crime thrillers and romantic comedies, namely: Confessions of An IT Employee, The Murder of Jay Shekhar and When I Find You. Her short stories are: The Code of Conduct In Her Shoes in Born Too Soon anthology and The Witch Of Strawhorn in Fantasia Divinity Magazine Issue 11. She is also a Columnist at The Post India and SheThePeople.tv where she writes articles about creativity, lifestyle and travel, and a Speaker at TED Circles Kolkata 2020. She also has worked with the celebrated filmmaker Mr. Saad Khan at First Action Studios.

She won the Coimbatore Literary Awards 2020 – Most Promising in General Fiction for her book, Confessions of an IT Employee. She was also awarded as one of the Top 100 Debut Authors of India 2018-19 for The Murder of Jay Shekhar. She has also been awarded the Global Women

Inspiration Awards 2021 for her literary accomplishments, and Top 30 Under 30 - NationWide Awards 2021 by Business Mint in the Author category. She has also been conferred the titles of Woman of The Month by Woman Times in March 2021. She is the winner of Sharing Stories Book Awards 2021 in the Romance category for her novel, Confessions of An IT Employee. She is also a recipient of the 1000 Women of Asia Award 2022 by Womennovator's in association with Consulate General of India, New York, Ministry of IT and Telecommunications, Government of India.

She was interviewed on various podcasts and in newspapers including Your Story Media, Daily Hunt, Zee5, Business Standard, ANI News, Eat My News, The Hans India, The FrontList Show, United Kingdom's International Radio Station- Chat and Spin Radio and on the American podcast – Inside The Minds of Authors with DC Gomez. A Software Engineer, a globetrotter and an avid reader, she has visited more than 14 countries. She has conducted various creative writing workshops such as Writing Skills Workshop for students of NPS, Mumbai and Delhi, and in Bangalore. She hopes to inspire youngsters to embrace their uniqueness through her books. She loves to interact with her readers on social media. You may also write to her at: pinkysawkar@gmail.com

Read more from the Author

The Murder of Jay Shekhar

Jay Shekhar is a travel buff, has an insatiable hunger for adventure and a strange quality of befriending men thirty years older than him. He lives in the suburbs of Bangalore. From encountering a surfing accident on the shores of Goa, to trekking the hills of Ramnagara, Jay is a tough nut to be knocked down.

Who is lurking in the woods of Ramnagara? Will Jay's habits ultimately cost him his life? Is love rekindled when two old flames come face to face? Does your fate depend on the company you keep?

Find out in this murky tale of lost love, jealousy and murder.

Read on Amazon Kindle

When I Find You

Nikhil catches a last-minute flight from Delhi to Bengaluru on a personal mission, but it is only the beginning. Will his journey bear fruit or be an utter waste of time?

Meanwhile, Vidya is meddling in matters she ought not to interfere in.

Can love be delusional? With dark secrets buried deep, who will win in this battle of wits?

Read on Amazon Kindle

Don't forget to **rate** and **review** Confessions of an IT Employee,
The Murder of Jay Shekhar and When I Find You
on **Amazon** and **Goodreads**!

Coming Soon (2024)

The Splintered Memories by Shalini P Sawkar

A serial killer on the loose. A young couple madly in love. A psychologist pushed to her limits.

We are all in search of that one great love—
one that feels comfortable yet exciting, noble yet downright dirty, one that will heal all the wounds of our pasts and set everything right, and upon finding which the treacherous paths that we treaded all along become worthwhile.

Mrigya, an art curator piecing together the fragments of her shattered heart, embarks on a journey of healing and self-discovery.

Lekh, CEO of a startup with a string of failed businesses and relationships, is on the verge of a breakthrough that could change the Indian social media landscape forever. Will he sabotage his career for a whirlwind, 'once-in-a-lifetime' kind of romance?

Anokha, a young psychologist and rising YouTube star, is determined to make her mark in the industry. Torn between her quest for success and the protection of her family, she is forced to confront the dark corners of her psyche.

As their paths intertwine, a thrilling game of love and secrets unfolds, leaving a trail of kisses and dead bodies. Delve into a captivating tale of passion, deception and the unwavering power of the human spirit to survive.

*